"*Great Disasters* is an elegiac and moving first novel. Chambers writes beautiful, precise prose that carefully narrates the story of his characters' high school years: reckless and callow, but also formative and tender. With great compassion and an evocative sense of place and history, Chambers captures the intricate ways adulthood is shaped by the long shadows of adolescence."

—Dana Spiotta,
author of *Wayward*

"Grady Chambers, poet, has written a tender, beautifully observed debut novel, an empathic recollection of becoming, of love and what it is made of. In Chambers's kind voice is wonder at it all. *Great Disasters* is great fiction."

—Christine Schutt,
author of *Pure Hollywood*

"*Great Disasters* is at once an artistic coming-of-age novel and a scathing indictment of our already fairly long American twenty-first century. Like a modern day Binx Bolling, Grady Chambers's warmhearted moviegoing narrator diagnoses an entire generation's moral and spiritual malaise, sparing himself least of all. The book is so inviting and entertaining that its ultimate emotional impact sneaks up on you."

—Christopher Beha,
author of *The Index of Self-Destructive Acts*

"*Great Disasters* is a beautiful debut novel that asks hard questions about the ways our earliest friendships shape, sustain, challenge, and change us. A narrator who refuses simple answers returns to the memories that haunt him most, knowing there is meaning to be found there, even if it's not the meaning he expects or can bear. The result is both heartbreaking and hopeful."

—Amber Caron,
author of *Call Up the Waters*

"*Great Disasters* is at once earnestly old-fashioned and quietly contemporary. Its narrator's account of his cohort of mostly privileged Chicago boys as willfully unselfconscious drinkers from middle school to middle age seems to track America's own dismal arc from 9/11 to the ascension of Trump. But the narrator's focus, for better and for worse, is always himself: his fears and sadnesses regarding his own meekness and inauthenticity, and the distance he maintains from those he claims to cherish. Even so, in his attempt to parse the past and face the truth he reminds us how much *is* available to us, if we only have the courage to choose it."

—Jim Shepard,
author of *Phase Six*

This is the story of how we became. I write those words but remain uncertain what they mean. . . . Drinking was a part of it. But as much as it was drinking, it was Ryan's love for Jana. And as much as it was Ryan's love for Jana, it was equally the war.

In the early 2000s in Chicago, six young men start high school. Though they've been friends since boyhood, their high school years set them on new paths: The wars in Iraq and Afghanistan begin, along with the protests against them; Ryan falls in love but struggles to hold onto it; and he and the others learn to lose themselves in alcohol. With each passing year—as they enter college or the military, then the world beyond; form new relationships with partners and children; and navigate shifting loyalties to a changing country—the narrator, Graham, feels the group breaking further apart and finds himself asking: What does it mean to move forward, both with and without one another?

Exploring the beauty, hope, and humor that can be found even in moments of deep loneliness and devastation, Grady Chambers's *Great Disasters* moves between memories of high school and early adulthood to consider friendship, first love, patriotism, protest, addiction, and more. An exquisitely written, profoundly moving debut novel, *Great Disasters* is an intimate portrait of disasters big and small, personal and political—and the ways the two are intertwined—and the announcement of a stunning new voice in American fiction.

Great Disasters

Great Disasters

a novel

Grady Chambers

Tin House

The characters and events in this book are fictitious. Any similarity to real persons, living or dead, is coincidental and not intended by the author.

Copyright © 2025 by Grady Chambers

Zando supports the right to free expression and the value of copyright. The purpose of copyright is to encourage writers and artists to produce the creative works that enrich our culture. Thank you for buying an authorized edition of this book and for comply- ing with copyright laws by not reproducing, scanning, uploading, or distributing this book or any part of it without permission. If you would like permission to use material from the book (other than for brief quotations embodied in reviews), please contact connect@zandoprojects.com.

Tin House is an imprint of Zando.
zandoprojects.com

First US Edition 2025
Manufacturing by Kingery Printing Company
Text and cover design by Beth Steidle

The publisher does not have control over and is not responsible for author or other third-party websites (or their content).

Library of Congress Cataloging-in-Publication Data
Names: Chambers, Grady, author.
Title: Great disasters : a novel / Grady Chambers.
Description: First US edition. | Portland, Oregon : Tin House, 2025.
Identifiers: LCCN 2025015229 | ISBN 9781963108507 (paperback) |
ISBN 9781963108569 (ebook)
Subjects: LCGFT: Novels.
Classification: LCC PS3603.H354 G74 2025 | DDC 813/.6—dc23/eng/20250428
LC record available at https://lccn.loc.gov/2025015229

10 9 8 7 6 5 4 3 2 1

Manufactured in the United States of America

Contents

Great Disasters

Freshman

In those years we lived like sisters. I almost wrote brothers—we were boys—but that doesn't feel accurate. We slept over. We shared clothes. We competed. We knew each other's bodies as I imagined sisters did. I saw this movie once with a hidden garden in it. I remember a group of sisters, the deep green of the garden walls, the cream of the girls' dresses. I'm afraid this won't make sense, but somehow in memory it mixes together—my own childhood, the garden in the movie, the girls hidden inside it—so that they've become somehow us; we left our sweatshirts, our T-shirts, our basketball shorts on the floors of one another's rooms, so that years later I wore Caesar's baseball shirt though I'd never even played, and Ryan wore David's graduation ring, though Ryan never managed to graduate, and when as young men we saw each other again, home for Thanksgiving, one of us might recognize another's jacket, or another's bracelet, and say, "Wasn't that mine once?" and none of us were really certain.

This is the story of how we became. I write those words but remain uncertain what they mean. We were friends as boys, then suddenly it was high school. Planes crashed into the World Trade Center. Ryan and Jana fell in love. We never would've used that word back then, but from this distance it is plain to me that there was love in what connected them.

All these years later and those two don't even speak, where once they sat beside each other on the bus each Sunday, riding it east through Chicago from Jana's parents' place, following Fullerton Avenue all the way to the lake. The rest of us lost touch with Ryan too, though somewhere in my apartment are things he once gave me: an American flag after he enlisted; a pair of silver cuff links he asked me to hold for safekeeping, long ago. I guess that's what this story is: Ryan's cuff links in my drawer, when I haven't heard his voice for years.

The summer before our freshman year of high school, Caesar and I spent two weeks at a hockey camp in upstate Michigan.

We hated it there. Up before the sun for a run, the path a beaten dirt track that wound through the thick woods.

It would still be dark when we started out. We were half-asleep, our muscles moaning as we jostled through the forest, still exhausted from the day before. But there was a beauty to it too: there was a quake we could hear in the green around us as we ran, everything that lived there just waking up. By night our necks were raw pink, our feet aching from skating all day, and we ate dinner under the cafeteria's grim fluorescents, hunched over our lunch trays, too tired to speak.

There was a goalie coach at the camp who—"whom," whatever, you know what I mean—Caesar made friends with, a twenty-eight-year-old from Romania who hated it there even more than we did. The last night of camp, he barged into our room with five Heinekens and an extra-large bag of Lay's potato chips. I finished my first beer before Caesar finished his, so the coach and I each got two while Caesar only got one. We were fourteen years old, and it wasn't the first time drinking for Caesar or me, but it was the first time we admitted to the other that we drank.

I guess you'll need to know that there were seven of us—me, Caesar, Ryan, Ben, Neil, Ricky, David. That's a lot of names to remember, but you can mostly forget about Ricky: he seemed to materialize whenever we were drinking, get drunk quicker than any of us, then completely disappear, toppled over in the flower beds or discovered the next morning passed out on someone's parents' basement floor. We'd pass him in the rush of the school hallway on Monday morning as he disappeared into the crowd, then find him beside us the following weekend, opening up another beer.

When Caesar and I got back from hockey camp, high school began. You know what that's like. But drinking came back with us, and suddenly there was this excitement in our life. We drifted from class to class. We made bridges out of toothpicks. We mapped the constellations onto a huge black tarp in science class, then turned it into a tent, and lay beneath it. We fell asleep in assembly, or at least Ryan always did. I sat beside him, entranced as I watched the girl in front of me trace shapes with her finger along the neck and shoulders of the girl who sat beside her.

What it was that lulled me I didn't know; maybe how gentle that gesture was, or maybe how it seemed impossible back then that I would ever be close enough with someone that they might let me touch them like that.

Fridays emerged through that haze like some beacon out at sea, growing brighter through the diminishing week. The bell tolled through the school at 3:30, and by 3:33 Caesar, Ryan, and I were already in the lobby. David always skipped off as soon as school ended to go to his mandolin lesson. Ben we called "Club Kid" because we couldn't keep up with all the after-school organizations he'd signed up for: the Sierra Club and Young Democrats and whatever other names kids give to the ways they want to save the world.

Ben had a good heart—he was kind through and through. As we zipped our backpacks, he'd appear out of the mass of people with his loping walk and rounded shoulders, his stiff thatch of brown hair jutting from his head like a shrub.

"Hey Greenpeace!" Ryan would yell. Or: "Hey Save the Zebras," he'd shout at Ben across the lobby. "Yo Ben! Yo Mahatma! Yo Mother Teresa! Call us when you're done!" he'd cry, laughing and waving his baseball cap at Ben's departing back.

But for all the shit Ryan gave him, Ryan was the one to cheer for him the loudest whenever one of Ben's clubs was presenting at assembly. Ryan, as you might have guessed, was beautiful: tall, tan, trim, with the whisper of a cleft lip that made it look like he was always just about to sneer or smile. He could do that whistle where you stick your pinkies in your mouth and the sound shoots out like a rocket. When Ben walked on stage, Ryan would lift himself to perch on his seat-back, his feet digging down into the cushion, his wolf whistle piercing the air so sharply every kid in there turned around to see who did it.

Each Friday, by early evening, David and Ben would arrive at Ryan's, Caesar and I would already be there, and Ryan's parents would be at the television, transfixed by the footage of the crashing planes, the brand-new war, the names of Afghan provinces suddenly on everyone's lips like they were places they'd been familiar with for years. We'd slip out the back door and prowl the block near Big Lake Liquors until we convinced a stranger to buy us beer.

It was easier than you'd think. We picked guys who looked like they'd just finished college. Most told us to fuck off, but one in ten would shrug and get us what we asked for.

There was a steel yard about a mile west of Ryan's house. It was strangely unprotected, and beautiful in this way I'd only seen before in movies. There's this French one called *Graduate First* where these teenage kids drift around some dead-end rural town. They drink too much; they party in abandoned houses; someone sleeps with someone they shouldn't; someone gets beat up.

It seemed like it was always winter in that movie, and I'd think of it as we slipped under the chain-link into the grounds of the steel yard. We were on the west side of the city, so you could see clear across Chicago, the brown brick shoulders of the factories leading like steps to the skyscrapers that shined in the distance.

The steel yard held huge tubes of steel sheeting, laid out in long straight rows, like submarines waiting to be sent out to sea. We'd sit in the windbreak made by the tubes, their curved sides curved against our spines, and spend all night making plans we knew would never happen: Ryan had heard from Jana that people were going to Ashley's. Ben had heard from Ricky that a girl from Saint Ignatius had keys to a cousin's empty house in Schaumburg, but that was in the suburbs, and how the hell were we going to get out there?

The plans we spoke of were always just a car ride or a party out of reach, and the truth is I didn't want any of those plans to happen anyway, even if they could. I was shy, though I was always trying to be as brash as Ryan was, and though I kept it a secret, I would sit there wondering what could be better than being exactly where we were, the six of us huddled together on the cold earth, out of the wind and drinking, imagining the versions of ourselves we thought we wanted to be, but not yet having to be them.

I'm going to go back in time for a moment. From somewhere else all our parents arrived in Chicago, and except for Caesar (his birth name was Eduardo but as a kid liked Little Caesars Pizza so much the name just stuck), it's the place where each of us was born. The city runs for twenty-two miles along the coast of Lake Michigan, and then the coast keeps going, leaving the city behind. To the east, the lake looms like an ocean. Most people outside the Midwest don't entirely understand how huge that lake is. In winter, the waves roll in like ships and pile against the shore, the water freezes as the winter deepens, and by January there are these great white mounds up and down the coastline, big as boulders but frozen and jagged, entirely composed of snow and ice, like something from an alien planet washed up on our shores.

When we were boys, Ryan and I woke to fresh snow one February morning. His parents were asleep, so we slipped out on our own. On the north side of the city, where Ryan lived at the time, these old brick apartment buildings sit right along the lake. One day they'll be eaten away by the weather or some great tidal wave arriving from the lake's far side, but that morning we left a shoe propped in his parents' front door so it wouldn't lock behind us, we crossed the frozen lot, we climbed over its rough wood rails, and then we were standing on the shore, the low sky gray and faceless as far as you could see.

Standing among those alien mounds of ice, as tall as four of me and wider than I could see around, I felt small. Snow had been falling for months, but the lake's wind had blown it into massive drifts, so in places the ground was strangely bare, and you could kick your toe down and hit soft brown clumps of sand and leaves. We stood there looking out while his parents were sleeping, the wind howling around us, just the ice and the sky in every direction, like we were the only ones on earth.

I have to keep reminding myself what the story is. There were all these separate threads that began our freshman year, though what they were building toward wouldn't become clear until we were so much deeper into our lives. It was like weavers beginning their work at different sides of a giant tapestry—the different threads meeting, many years later, to reveal the broader picture.

Drinking was a part of it. But as much as it was drinking, it was Ryan's love for Jana. And as much as it was Ryan's love for Jana, it was equally the war.

We were hockey players. I know I've said that, but it was 2001, and all that fall and winter, before the ref would drop the puck, both teams gathered at the center of the ice. As the national anthem played over the speakers, we stood in a circle, arm in arm with the boys from the other team, our heads bowed as the announcer asked us to close our eyes and remember, in silence, the lives lost on September 11.

I remember how tinny the music sounded, how high and insubstantial as it floated, each weekend, through the space of those cold arenas. Barrington, Glencoe, Winnetka, Highland Park: in the suburbs that surrounded us, white and wealthy, lawn flags with the stars and stripes stood beside signs that said, "These Colors Don't Run."

Later, I'd see the irony in that: it wouldn't be *their* sons who would fight that war, and except for Ryan, it wouldn't be us either. But at that time, September 11 was only a couple of months behind us. Bombs were already dropping on Afghanistan. Everything that was happening was happening so fast.

In truth, I was excited by the war. My parents were activists—civil rights, anti-violence, more on that later—but with my eyes shut in the ice rinks in the suburbs, observing another moment of silence, I felt this strange swell of emotion: with the lights turned off, standing in the quiet, hand in hand in the circle of boys, it felt like we were being initiated into something more adult.

The sunny day, the planes plunging into the ribs of the tall gray towers. In the dark arena, standing beside Ryan, with the spotlit flag hanging on the ice rink wall, it felt like something had been done to us; like we were the ones who had experienced tragedy, though none of us had been touched by it.

I never would've admitted that to my parents: the swell I felt in my chest as I swayed among the boys before our games. And it's strange to say it now, but I see that, looking back, part of what I felt on that September morning wasn't just the horror that everyone always tells you about, but also something like relief: something had happened. It hadn't happened to me—that was plain to me. It hadn't happened to us, though we were told what happened had happened to all of us. It hadn't happened to me, but I was expected to grieve. It's strange to write this, but after the planes hit, life didn't seem as boring as it had.

To understand the impact of what would go on to happen our senior year, it's important that you understand Ryan's love for Jana. But for you to understand that, I have to tell you about Sam, my middle-school girlfriend. That probably sounds weird, but what I mean is that I'd been in eighth grade when we met—Sam was still in seventh—and we stayed together for the first few months that I was in high school. My friends teased me endlessly for dating a middle schooler, but Sam had a sister in the senior class, and when her sister threw a party our freshman fall, Sam agreed to keep it secret from their mom, on the condition that my friends and I would be invited too.

The night of the party, we arrived early. We stood in the hallway of Sam's apartment building, holding as much beer as we could carry. Sam was my girlfriend, but I hoped her sister would be the one to open the door. I think I hoped that seeing us with the beer, she'd view us as more mature than the freshmen that we were, somehow older and more adult.

We held the twelve-packs in our arms like treasure, and Sam's sister *did* appear when the door swung open. But she was on the phone, her hair wet from the shower and wrapped in a towel, stacked like a beehive, and she quickly shooed us into a little den off the kitchen, then closed the door behind us. As the night deepened we sat quarantined in the dim den, drinking from our warming pile of beers, listening to the sound of the apartment filling with people on the other side of the den's closed doors.

All evening, I watched, not understanding, as Sam's expression darkened. We were playing a game called Kings. We sat around a scarred wooden table, Jana beside Ryan, Ben and Caesar at a spot at each end.

Ryan was in good spirits. Drinking wasn't dark to us then, and freshman year, with Jana nearby, Ryan became the person I'd always hoped that drinking would make me: convivial and easy, funny and carefree, one thing flowing freely to the next.

That was one of Jana's effects on him—he didn't seem to drink as much when she was there. And so, that year, he embodied for a while the things that in our lives, in our future as drinkers, we'd seek and rarely achieve: congeniality where we'd later find confusion; easy conversation where we'd later find silence; an ease in ourselves, whereas years later we'd finish a sixth drink, then a seventh, and stare inward in silence and bewilderment.

At some point in the night—it was late October—Ryan started to pretend he was a vampire. I looked over at Sam, who was looking at Ryan. We watched him sneak up behind Jana, and as she was halfway through telling us a story, he pretended to sink his fangs into her neck. She squealed and squirmed, but she was laughing.

She howled, her hands reaching back to pry him off.

"It is I," he said, growling like he was Nosferatu or something. "Dracu-Ryan."

"That sounds like an insurance product," Jana scoffed, tossing him off her.

"Mhmmm. That's right," he growled again, wrapping his arms around her. "I'll insure you for eternity."

When I think about the event that happened our senior year, the prank we played and the way it shifted—without us knowing it—the lives we were headed toward, I sometimes remember that night at Sam's, and the sense I had—observing Ryan and Jana—that I was witnessing the early days of a love that was fierce in its seriousness, large in its feeling.

All night we kept drinking. We played Kings, we pulled cards, we touched the floor, we pointed at the ceiling, we drank beer in long cold gulping pulls. As the night got later, Sam grew quieter and quieter. Ryan kept leaning over between games so his head rested in Jana's lap, his voice and laughter carrying up to us from beneath the table the more he drank.

Though the specifics have grown hazy, I remember Sam looking over at me, holding my eyes, staring intently, like she was searching for something. Then she abruptly got up from the table. I followed after her, and as we passed into the hallway, she pulled me into the bathroom. When she turned her face to me, she was crying.

I sat on the toilet's flipped-down lid. I reached for Sam's hand. She let me. I wrapped my arms around her waist, bringing her close. I laid the side of my face against her stomach. She stood above me, holding me against her, her sobs heaving with her breath.

"I know you don't love me like that," she finally said.

"Like what?" I asked, though I already knew what she meant.

"The way Ryan loves Jana," she said.

She breathed in hard then, wiping her nose with the back of her hand, while I kept my face pressed against her.

For all his faults, Ryan was always older than his years. Not in a soul-level way: he wasn't wise; he was often thoughtless; he was never particularly kind. But what existed between him and Jana never seemed childish. I remember arriving at his house one Friday to find the two of them sprawled on his living room couch. Ryan was on his back, holding a magazine in his hands that he pitched like a canopy above him as he read, while Jana breathed evenly, her head resting on Ryan's stomach, sleeping in the early dusk.

Even more than their Sunday bus rides to the lake, even more than hearing them one night—though they tried to be as quiet as possible, Jana's soft moan audible through the door I stopped to press my ear against—that was what astonished me: the two of them together in the evening, Jana sleeping against Ryan, so at ease with one another they didn't even need to speak.

I saw a movie once where Katharine Hepburn goes to Venice. She follows the sound of the bells to Piazza San Marco. She sits at a café. She's there alone; she's lonely; she's getting older. She smiles as she waves goodbye to people leaving on a boat, but when she turns her face, you can see that she is crying. I'm reminded of her now, thinking of the way Sam's face looked that night—her lower lip pouted and trembling, her whole body shaking as she tried to keep herself from weeping. It was one of the saddest things I'd ever seen.

I no longer recall what I said to Sam in that bathroom as she wept, but I know that I would've felt accused by what she'd said, and I know that I held her close to me so that she couldn't see my face, and I know that I denied the thing that she was saying to me. And though I denied it, Sam and I would be together only a few weeks longer, because I knew that what she'd said—that I didn't love her the way Ryan loved Jana—was true.

It was a strange time. All fall, bombs fell on Kabul. Light rain and a grey mist descended on Chicago the first week of November. By the second week, the Taliban fled, and Kabul was in the hands of the Northern Alliance. In the computer room at school, killing time until hockey practice, we peered over Ryan's shoulder as he clicked *play* on a pixilated video he said had been filmed by militants in Afghanistan.

"See that?" he asked, pausing the frame and pointing to something in the corner, gray and indistinct. Something about its shape made me think of the massive stone water cribs that sit like stationary ships off the shore of Lake Michigan and transfer water from the lake to the pumping stations and purification plants, until it winds up in the city's taps.

"That's about to get fucking blitzed by a missile," said Ryan, tapping at the gray thing wavering on the screen. Then he clicked *play* again, and it did, crumbling in a sudden eruption of fire, dust, pillars of black smoke.

I thought the video would end there, but it kept going. We could hear a voice off-screen. A man was speaking, and another man was speaking back. The camera suddenly jerked down, so the video showed a pair of feet, gravel, the feet in motion, fabric—maybe the man's pants or tunic—swishing across the frame. Then the feet stopped moving and the perspective jerked up, showing again the pillars of smoke, only now the smoke and the burning structure were much much closer. The camera swung around, and for a second I could see part of the face of the man who was filming: he was speaking directly into the camera, but holding it too close to him, so all you could see was his beard and teeth, and his tongue and throat when he spoke. Then the camera swung again and the burning structure was visible once more, and coming closer.

I found the video startling. As it continued, I sort of drifted back, edging toward the computer-room door. I think what frightened me was the firsthand perspective suggested by the graininess of the film. It felt fundamentally different from the livestreams of the war they showed each night on CNN and that I watched beside my parents, sitting in the living room. This video, its graininess, its handheld quality: what made me nervous was its intimacy. It was like a husband filming a wife, together in their bedroom, or a child who's discovered a camera in a drawer, and turns it on.

I was acutely aware of the living person behind the camera, filming. It made me feel at their mercy, in their hands. As they walked toward the burning structure, as Ryan continued to watch, I left the room. I didn't think I wanted to see what they might choose to show me next.

Hockey season was in full swing. Caesar, Ryan, and I made varsity as freshmen, and our weekends were filled with long rides to games in the northern suburbs, a caravan of fans trailing along in the buses behind us.

At our high school, hockey mattered. That's how Ryan met Sidney and Caesar met Latisha, though everyone called her Tish. They were seniors. They threw big parties. They came to every game. I walked out of the locker room after we beat Barrington one Saturday and saw the four of them together, talking by the water fountains. Sidney had a high black ponytail and chewed pink bubble gum, and before she and Tish departed, though he hadn't even asked, she unwrapped and placed a fat square piece in the palm of Ryan's hand, the gum still chalky from its wrapper.

Around that time, Jana had a pregnancy scare. The day the test came back negative, Ryan paraded through the freshman hallway, whooping like a cowboy as he rode on Caesar's back. Everyone just assumed he was excited because he'd managed to pass his geometry test, but on Friday evening, prying open a can of Coors, glowing with relief, he told us she'd been a week late, then two, until they'd both been convinced she'd need an abortion. They'd finally mustered the courage to go into CVS together and buy a test, and had used up all six sticks just to be certain the negative was true.

"You know, if she was though, and wanted to have it," he said to us shyly. "Not now, obviously. I just mean with her. If I was going to have one with anyone, I'd want it to be with her."

Jana danced. I can't believe it's taken me this long to tell you that. She was a ballerina ("I dance ballet," she always corrected us). We made a joke of that for a while, remembering our own sisters' childhood pageants, little girls in sparkly tiaras, until we saw Jana dance in the Pageant of the Twelve Days.

The pageant took place each year the night before Christmas break. The seniors did an elaborate skit, the a cappella groups did a sing-off for the Golden Cup, and the chorus kids held candles and sang hymns into the dim auditorium, the soft songs solemn and moving, though I never would have admitted that then. I slumped beside Ryan and Caesar, pretending I wasn't interested, but chills would ripple down the back of my neck as the singers got to the end of the final hymn, the voices of the chorus dropping out one by one until there was only a lone voice left, singing out into the dark.

There'd been rehearsals for a month, and it was tradition that the best act was saved for last. So we all sat up when the MC—the Snowdrop Queen, a girl from the senior class with a silver wand and a flowing gown—announced that it was a freshman who would close the pageant.

Ryan hadn't told us that Jana was a part of this, and when she took the stage she looked transformed, her waterfall of red hair impossibly tamed into the interlocking braids crowning the face of the girl before us, illuminated in a white beam of light.

From the darkness of the wings, a violin began to play, and Jana began to dance. She moved from left to right across the stage. She seemed completely without affectation, like someone might dance alone in their room. She moved with the deliberateness and gentleness of rain I'd once seen in an old movie I watched with my mother.

In the film, a girl is searching for her lost cat. It's nighttime in a dark alley, the girl's dress is soaked through. The way Jana danced—her feet so light she appeared to be almost without weight—made me think of the fabricated rain—fine and thin as needles—that seemed to follow the girl in the film as she searched in the alley, moving with her as she moved.

We were young enough that we'd never seen it before: someone so good at the thing they did that a kind of silence took hold of everyone in the auditorium, the reverence—whether you truly understood what you were looking at or not—of people witnessing something rare, or holy.

While Caesar and I snuck sips from a flask of Jim Beam, passing it between us, Ryan watched Jana with an attention I'd never seen him give anyone. He watched her like a teacher might observe a student trying to solve an equation on a chalkboard, wanting her to succeed. He knew her routine. He was following along. He watched her with nervousness and hopefulness.

I recognized the care of that attention. It was the same way I used to watch my sister during her ice-skating competitions—already knowing the places of risk, the point in the routine where she'd fallen in the past, trying to urge her through the challenge as I watched. Watching Ryan, I realized that what he felt toward Jana was different from anything the rest of us claimed to feel for the girls we'd dated. None of us had the language to come out and say it, so what we knew we knew from seeing in one another's behavior. And later, when I'd think of times I felt I'd witnessed love, I'd remember Ryan watching Jana dance, helpless to help her, though she clearly didn't need it, but anxious nonetheless, trying to silently will her through.

Two weeks after beating Barrington, when I'd left the locker room and watched from a distance as Sidney placed that block of chalky gum in Ryan's palm, I found myself fourteen floors above the earth, swaying before a window, trying to steady the blur as I looked out at the city from Tish's mother's apartment in the sky. Sidney had picked Ryan as her favorite, and Tish picked Caesar, and the rest of us got to come along for the ride. We'd arrived at Tish's door with our ragged duffel packed with a mishmash of warm beers. Sidney had laughed when Ryan offered her one, said, "Don't even bother," and flicked open a kitchen cabinet.

I could see what she meant. Inside, lined up like bowling pins, were trim bottles of wine, whiskey, gin, tequila—whatever you could want. And the fridge was the same: cold rows of Coronas and Heinekens that fizzed and hissed when we opened them, and we opened them again and again.

I remember that room so well. So many nights that winter, when everyone else was in the living room, I'd find myself alone for a moment in the kitchen in the dark, sent to get another round of beers, swaying a little as I reached for the refrigerator door, the yellow light when I opened it spilling across the cold white tile floor. From January until the spring dance, when things came apart, we spent at least one night every couple of weekends drinking from that endless well.

I don't know what Ryan told Jana. Maybe that he was at Caesar's house, or that we'd all gone to the movies, but every time we went to Tish's, one of us would end up so drunk by 10:00 PM that the others would put him in the bathtub to help him sober up. David had read somewhere that a bath was the quickest remedy for drunkenness, or at least the quickest path to seeming sober, so that's what we did. Whoever got sick, we'd run the water while he threw up into the toilet, then plunge him into the tub for a half hour or forty-five minutes, however long we could keep him there without him missing curfew.

Shots of tequila, four or five beers downed in an hour—we never learned our lesson. Sometimes it was me in the tub, but mostly it was Ryan. He'd lie naked in the water, one arm slung over the tub's pink edge, his head resting on the ledge, groaning like someone in a deep fever.

Ryan was beautiful, though I know I've already said that. Caesar, David, Ben, and Neil—each of them was. I know, I know, "everyone is," like Ben kept saying every time he got back from one of his ten thousand after-school clubs (Healthy Perspectives, in this case), but I mean they *really* were, and Ryan *really* was. I'd just seen *The 400 Blows* for the first time, and Ryan was like the child lead, nonchalant and easy in himself, willowy but trim as a Roman sheath.

In the bath, as soon as he felt better, he'd turn into a kid, scooping soap bubbles onto his head like a hat, arcing water out from his mouth like a fountain. And if it was Ryan who ended up there more than me, it was only because I was shy of undressing in front of others, whereas he and Caesar would strip without thought, demanding crackers, a can of seltzer, another beer, company, unembarrassed in their bodies as they floated face-up in the pale green.

That very first night there, swaying before the window, downtown's lights shined like champagne, slippery and golden. Somewhere behind me, Tish was sprawled with Caesar on the couch; David was asleep in the carpet, so drunk he'd rolled himself inside it. Sidney had bet Ryan that Ryan wasn't strong enough to hold her up, and she was in the air above the living room floor, spread out like an airplane, crying with laughter as Ryan, flat on his back, held her aloft, his feet supporting her stomach.

The kitchen counter was covered with empty bottles, crushed plastic cups, and cut limes, and amid that mess, Ryan's phone kept glowing and going dark. I didn't look, but I was certain it was Jana calling, and I worried when I looked over and saw Sidney's hair, freed from its ponytail, almost touching Ryan's face as she floated above him.

In the end, nothing really happened. Caesar made out with Tish. We unrolled David from the carpet. Ryan tapped out a message on his phone, then lay on the floor as Sidney dropped gummi bears into his waiting mouth.

Nothing really happened, but when it was time for us to go, Sidney brought her face so close to Ryan's that the bubble she blew with her chewing gum popped when it touched his nose, then she turned him around and pushed him out the door. Instead of leaving, we rode the elevator up to the eightieth floor, down to the second, then back up again. Caesar tried to break into the Sky-Gym, David spilled a beer on the elevator carpet, and then the fun was over when the elevator doors opened and the doorman appeared and curtly escorted us out.

Nothing really happened, but I could tell that Ryan felt guilty. On Monday morning, I arrived at school to find him on the bench outside the freshmen lockers, Jana sitting on one of his knees, Ryan's arms wrapped around her, his face resting against her back. For the next two days he kept coming up to her between classes, checking in, hovering like a hummingbird would hover over something it wants, or wants to protect, as if he was frightened to let her get too far outside his sight.

We had almost made it to the end of the year when the spring dance arrived. I say "we," though now that phrasing seems imprecise to me, or tenuous: so often I felt apart from them, or like I had to labor to be included. On Friday evenings, sitting in Ryan's basement, playing video games, what I felt, more than anything, was anxious—to say something funny, to stay in the flow of conversation, to prove myself worthy, in some way, to be among them. Part of that came from how they'd treated me when I'd been together with Sam. They'd never made an effort to include her. Whether because she was younger, or because she didn't have the social status they did, I wasn't sure. But if I spent a weekend night with her rather than with them, there might be repercussions: a coldness at school on Monday morning, or plans for the next weekend that didn't include me. It had separated me from them. It made me see how quickly their friendship could be withdrawn.

The first Friday of May, the school's halls blooming with sunlight, all the windows lifted open. The day was green and cool—summer was in the breeze—and so beautiful even the teachers seemed transformed. They seemed kinder, more yielding, less stern than their job typically required them to be.

We hardly had to beg and Ms. Paige let us have math class on the soccer field. We sat in a circle at its center, the lesson plan long abandoned, all of us talking about that evening's dance and the Varsity Barbecue that would happen on Saturday. Even Ms. Paige leaned back as she listened, her brown hair let down, her elbows resting on the grass, her hands—just like ours were—brushed with the field's black dirt.

Seeing her that way was a comfort. It made her seem like a person we could know, not just a teacher. It seemed like a reminder that the true world lay outside the school's doors. It seemed like a reminder that as large as our troubles there—a missed class, a failed test, something cruel that someone said—sometimes weighed on us, there was something bigger outside it all, something more important, and that we were making our way toward it.

My mom and dad were going out after work, so I knew we'd have the house to ourselves before the dance. When the bell rang at the end of the day, my friends went home, changed their clothes, and then came over. Ryan brought a half bottle of Captain Morgan, Caesar had a bag full of warm Bud Lights we threw in the freezer to get cold quickly, and we dug around in the basement storage room, taking whatever was dustiest and had alcohol in it, figuring if it was old my parents might not notice that it had gone missing.

There was a little back deck that extended off the kitchen. Ryan set up the speakers so the music played through the kitchen's open windows, and we sat at the deck table in the early evening, each with a freezing beer and a coffee mug filled with some mix of the stuff we'd stolen from the basement.

It's hard to fully describe how good it felt. The sky was pure blue. Birds chirped from their perches on the different wires crisscrossing the alley behind the house. Our music played steadily from the kitchen, but there was music everywhere: up and down the street, neighbors had come out into their backyards. Fires were lit, people laughed, barbecue smoke drifted through the air, lawn chairs were dug out of garages, brushed off and spread open for the first time in months, the hum of cicadas rose and fell, screen doors slammed shut, children's voices ricocheted in the dusk.

Ryan had a pack of cigarettes; we each opened a second beer, and then a third, and the blue smoke of the cigarettes rose into the deeper blue above us. Ben found a tennis ball in the basket by the back door. Perched on the railing on one side of the deck, he threw the ball to David, sitting on the railing opposite, and all evening they tossed it over the table, back and forth, forth and back, so when I think of that night, I remember leaning back in my chair and staring up into the wideness of the evening sky, the yellow ball arcing across it.

We hadn't meant to drink as much as we did. Jana was supposed to meet us, but her dance lesson was in the suburbs, and she called early on to say the traffic was bad trying to get back to the city.

Time was moving strangely. She called at six, but suddenly it was eight. Caesar made us tequilas mixed with Hawaiian Punch,

Ben won some convoluted bet, so he took just one shot of vodka while the rest of us took two, then Ryan reached into his back-pack and came out with a bottle of champagne he'd stolen from his parents.

Jana kept calling as darkness fell, wanting to meet up, but each time Ryan answered the phone he was less and less lucid. Each of us was. By the fifth call, Jana was trying to keep him on track, but Ryan was talking about other things altogether.

When I think back to it now, it was like a dream where you're trying to constantly catch up: Jana was already home, but Ryan kept telling her to call him when she got home from ballet. She'd left home to go to the school dance, but Ryan kept telling us she was coming to meet us.

By the eighth or ninth call, all he could manage to say was how much he loved her. She was asking him something else, but I remember how he just kept telling her that. It was like she wasn't even there, and he was talking to himself.

Eventually the phone simply dropped from his hand, and instead of picking it up, he left it there where it fell on the deck, and turned to us, slurring, then went on talking, like he'd forgot-ten he'd just been on the phone.

The music was booming through the school gymnasium when we arrived. It seemed like the whole high school was already there. The windows were steamed from the heat, and the room went white then dark from the pulse of a strobe light. Huge speakers loomed beneath the north basketball hoop, as wide and tall as newsstands. The booze had left us unsteady, stumbling, weaving as we walked, like someone woozy from a punch, but it hardly mattered: bodies were so crammed in that gym that we were held upright as we moved into the crush, jostling forward like people in a subway car.

I began to feel it had been a mistake to come. The room trembled from the music, you couldn't tell who was who in the darkness, and suddenly the possibility of being found out by one of the teachers chaperoning the dance seemed very real: they stood on the risers ringing the gymnasium and at each of the exits. Out of the darkness a hand shot out and grabbed my shoulder.

"Where the fuck have you guys been? Jana's going to murder him."

I could make out the face of Jana's best friend, Devon. She was shouting into my ear, screaming to be heard over the music, nodding her head in the direction behind me, where I figured Ryan must be.

I was trying to say something in return, but suddenly each word felt complexly formed, bulky and unwieldy as I tried to answer, my mind weirdly trained on how strange and stiff my mouth felt attempting to make language make sense.

Devon shook her head and pulled me closer, pointing to her ear to say she couldn't hear me. The flashing lights were casting everything in a procession of changing colors.

"Your skin is so blue!" was all I managed.

"Where is Ryan?" she shouted back.

I pointed behind me, but she took me by the shoulders and turned me where I'd pointed, and Ryan wasn't there.

"Come on," she said, grabbing my wrist, trying to force her way through the crowd.

I stumbled along as she dragged me behind her, her head lowered to push past the scrum of backs and shoulders and the mass of bent heads heaving as people danced. And suddenly we were down at the far end of the gym, underneath the basket, to the side of the throbbing speakers.

Outside their direct path, it felt like we'd found a pocket of quiet, and I leaned against the speakers with my eyes closed, trying to steady myself against the pulse and flash of the strobe lights and the feeling that the room was spinning around me.

"Drink this," Devon said, and freezing water spilled down my chin as I tried to both sip and say thank you at once.

I closed my eyes again.

After a few minutes, I felt my hat lift off my head and when I looked up, I saw it bobbing in the air above me, a makeshift flag Devon waved above the mass of people around us, and then in a moment there was Jana's red hair, and there was Jana herself, pushing toward us.

Devon had her phone in her hands, and tilted the screen toward Jana when she got to us.

"It keeps going straight to voicemail," Devon said.

"You're here from dance?" I slurred at Jana, wobbling off to the left.

"Is Ryan here?" she asked me. "Did he come in with you?"

I nodded and leaned back again against the speakers, grateful that I didn't need to try to speak.

"Try him again?" Devon said to Jana, but just then a roar went up from somewhere near the center of the gym.

We turned to look. Bars of blue light rained down, and cheers rose again from the basketball court's center, cheers and catcall whistles, but we couldn't see anything beyond the heave and sway of people jumping to the beat with raised arms.

Devon nodded her head in that direction and Jana went after her. I trailed behind them, trying to keep up.

There must've been eight hundred people in that gym. A mess of confetti stars in green and yellow covered the basketball court, sliding around under everybody's feet, pulsing with the thrum from the speakers.

Yellow for spring, I remember thinking, as I stared down where the toes of my sneakers waded through the confetti.

The whoops and howls got louder as we got closer to the center circle. A disco ball was strung above it, so you could see the faces more clearly there. As Devon cleared a path, I saw that it was mostly upperclassmen: the soccer captain with luau wreaths draped around his neck; the Snowdrop Queen from the Pageant of the Twelve Days perched piggyback on the shoulders of her friend. They were all crowded at the court's center, whooping as they danced, circling around something that was happening there, like children in a schoolyard will make a wall around two boys shoving each other, getting ready to fight.

Through the gaps of their bodies, I saw suddenly the shiny blue of Ryan's polyester jacket. It shimmered in the glow of the strobes, and for an instant I felt a flood of relief pass through me, and then confusion. It was definitely his jacket—I could see the silver lion climbing up its back—but it wasn't Ryan who was wearing it. It hung broad and loose across the shoulders of a slim girl with black hair. She had her arms wrapped around the shoulders of the person she danced with, his face buried in her hair where it fell at her neck. From behind him another set of hands emerged, lifting the boy's face up and back. The face was Ryan's, his jacket was on Tish's shoulders as he danced with her, and the hands when the strobe light passed across them belonged to Sidney. She danced at Ryan's back, turning his face toward hers as the whistles and cheers rose into a pitch, and then her mouth, as Jana stood there watching, was on his.

Palm Springs

Over spring break my junior year of college, I left Pomona and took a bus to Palm Springs to spend a week in the desert. Ostensibly I was there to do research toward my senior thesis. I'd written a paper on the way the Bush administration had sold the wars to the American public. It won a departmental prize, and with the prize came $3,000 that was supposed to give me the resources to expand the paper into a thesis.

It seemed great in theory, but the truth is I didn't know what I was doing. The day I got the award, I sat across from my advisor in her cramped campus office while she talked like a speed addict about all these different institutes and specialized libraries I should use the money to travel to visit. I nodded along, pretending to jot down the name of one scholar or another as they streamed right by me into some future version of the paper I'd never successfully complete. The more I tried to expand it in the months after that meeting, the more uncertain I became of what I was trying to say. Now the year was ending, I'd hardly spent a dollar of the prize money, and so I set up a few interviews with professors at UC Palm Springs, used some of the cash to buy a plane ticket for my girlfriend, Nina, and convinced her to fly in from Cleveland at the end of the week (she'd been visiting her parents there) to join me in the desert for UC Palm Springs' annual party, the Spring Fling.

But there was a hiccup. My mom bought a ticket from Chicago to come out to meet me. She told me she'd always wanted to see the desert, but I suspect now that she was worried about me, and wanted to see my face so she could determine just how worried she should be.

That semester I'd been kicked out of one dorm and was on probation in another. In the scope of things I hadn't done anything all that serious: in broad strokes, my infraction involved drinking, a French maid Halloween outfit, and a failed sprint away from campus security (darkness, lawn ornaments). But where before I'd called my parents every Sunday to check in, the distance between calls had been steadily getting longer, and my mom wanted to see for herself what was going on.

How lonely and sad the desert was. On the bus ride there, I kept looking up from the article I was rereading as part of my research to peer out at the endless mounds of white sand, relentless and barren, accumulating like dread. The article had been published two springs before. It was the one about Iran by Seymour Hersh that ran in *The New Yorker* and freaked everybody out, or at least all the teachers in Pomona's poli-sci department. It had warned about officials in the Bush Administration and secret plans for war with Iran. I had encountered it when it was first published, but reading it again I felt a growing dread the more I read. The gist of it was that officials were convinced Iran wouldn't stop until it had a nuclear weapon, and that the US military would prevent that from happening at any cost. Secret sources said a list of targets had already been drawn up—presumably the list still existed and was at the ready—and all the president would need to do was give a nod of his head and the bombing would begin.

Ryan's marine unit was stationed in Afghanistan by the time I took that trip to Palm Springs—how he ended up in the marines

I'll get to later—but if I'm honest I don't think he even entered my mind that day. The bus rolled through the darkening desert. The fear I felt seemed large, and existential. The landscape around me looked like the end of the earth. The piece made it seem like the whole planet was in peril.

And it was, of course—I mean it is—but that day, annihilation felt imminent, and entirely likely. It is also true that before getting on the bus, I had been drinking for three consecutive nights. I was shaking from it, from tiredness and dehydration. On top of that, I'd singed off locks of my hair bending down to light a cigarette off a friend's lit stove, so Nina had buzzed my head, and I still hadn't figured out how I was going to explain that to my mother.

The motel where my mom was staying was called the Palm Sundae. It was on a side street that teed off from Palm Springs' busy neon stretch. You can probably picture that motel because you've seen it a thousand times: a modernist version of the standard formula, a thin scrim of chain-link separating the parking lot from a small swimming pool, glowing blue in the deepening evening. As my cab pulled up, I looked out to see a bright sign dwarfing the low motel, neon-green palm fronds sprouting, inexplicably, from an ice-cream sundae.

What I remember most from that week is going to see movies with my mom. *The Visitor*, *Paranoid Park*, *The Other Boleyn Girl*, *My Blueberry Nights*. It was too hot to do anything else. The movie theater was in some awful desert mall, one of those sprawling complexes of chain restaurants and brand-name clothing stores all selling variations of the same basic outfit. Mannequins in blue button-downs and pastel khakis stared blindly into the dusk, their white faces eyeless and smooth as marble, imprisoned behind the plate-glass windows. Every time I glanced in at them

I caught sight of myself, startled to see my own thin face looking back at me in the gleam of the clean windows, my shorn skull as stark and bare as the heads of the vacant mannequins.

I was scared. That's imprecise, but it's the plainest way to say it. I felt far away from the people I loved. It didn't make sense—my mother was right there—but I'd think of Nina, or think of my father, or think of my sister, or even my mother, sitting in front of me, and feel suddenly and inexplicably frightened for them.

I was scared for myself too, though at that time I couldn't say why. I sat across the table from my mother on the second floor of a chain Italian place, my bowl of pasta hardly touched, looking out the broad windows at the bands of color the sunset had left in the sky over the low row of hills to the west.

Many years later, sitting with my mother after dinner in my parents' kitchen, my face would collapse in tears when she unexpectedly reached her hand out and asked me what was wrong. I didn't even know I'd been holding them back. But there in the desert, silently telling myself not to have another drink, I just shook my head when she asked the same question.

"I don't think anything's wrong," I said. "Why? Am I quiet?" She laughed.

"You're always quiet. But you've barely said a word. And you haven't eaten anything."

"I'm a little nervous," I said.

"About the interviews?"

"A little bit," I said.

Earlier, as the waiter had led us to the table, I'd excused myself to use the bathroom. I'd leaned over the sink in front of the row of bright mirrors, splashing water on my burning face. I ran my soaked hands along the back of my neck. Mushroom clouds; bunker busters burrowing a thousand feet beneath the earth before they exploded; my incoherent paper; the pile of my burnt hair in the middle of the kitchen floor. Everything I was worried about felt like it had arrived at once.

"Do you want to talk about it?" my mother asked me at the table, as if she could read my thoughts. But she'd meant the interviews.

I shook my head.

"I'll prepare tonight," I said. "It'll all go fine."

But when the waiter came over and asked if I'd like more wine, I looked into my empty glass, and even as my mother reached across the table to cover its top, I shrugged and told him, "Yes."

The next morning I went to meet Rand Davis for our interview. The collar of the button-down I'd picked to wear was yellow from sweat. My mother noticed, and made me change. The only formal piece of clothing I had left was a crumpled cardigan I'd worn on the bus, and as I sat across from Rand at a Starbucks on the strip—freezing air pouring down on us from the cranked-up AC—I noticed I kept running a hand down the cardigan's sleeves and breast, trying and failing to disappear the wrinkles.

My advisor had looked tired when I told her I had plans to interview a handful of people, one of who was Rand Davis.

"Whom," she said, "not who," a lesson I never seemed able to learn. "And Rand's a pundit," she sighed, "not a scholar."

But his op-eds were in line with the argument my paper was making!

"That's part of your problem!" She was nearly yelling with exasperation. "You shouldn't be arguing anything!"

That was what she kept telling me, that I was "proactively projecting." She loved that term.

"You should be gathering evidence," she finally said, letting out another sigh. "Sort through it, see where it leads you. Let it tell you its own conclusions."

We were seniors in high school when Ryan enlisted. Sitting in that Starbucks in Palm Springs, how long had it been since I'd seen him? Almost two years, I figured, counting back, though the distance between us felt much larger. All I knew of his life by then came from the status updates he posted to Facebook, shorthand fragments I squinted at in the glow of my screen, unable to sleep, trying to decipher them, like a child sitting at the top of the stairs, straining to make sense of their parents' argument.

> 09/05/06, 7:41 AM: *Just landed in San Diego!*
> 01/07/07, 11:53 PM: *0500 for laps at Camp Pendleton*
> 07/15/07, 4:18 AM: *balls deep in recon county—sayonara for now, probably for a while*

I pored over the grainy pictures: Ryan in a line of men, gripping his gun in a vertical hold. Ryan in camo, sunglassed and kneeling, smoke rising off a dusty road. A headshot of Ryan in some kind of yearbook—Machine Gunner, "CAB," 4th Marines. Those were the words printed in white beneath the photo of him.

It was disorienting. It was like the boy I'd known had found a way to wriggle free from the life we'd shared and had stepped into another, and from that parallel path—so near but impossible to cross, in a uniform as crisp and tight as a straitjacket—he was now staring back at me.

The last time I'd seen him was the summer after my first year of college. It had been the summer after my first year of college. It was a hot day, late August. I'd left the congressman's office where I worked as an intern, licking envelopes and answering phones, trying to assure whoever I was speaking to that the congressman agreed with them.

The heat, even in the early evening, had been thick and heavy. It rose off the blacktop where a sea of cars, impossibly bright in the sweltering density, stretched down the avenue as far as I could see. The heat seemed to shimmer off the vehicles.

I picked up Caesar, then we picked up Ryan.

At the time of our high school graduation he'd been six credits shy of what he needed. The principal let him walk with the rest of the class, but the diploma he'd been handed contained a blank sheet of card stock, whereas ours held a certificate of graduation. The summer ended, and he never made the credits up. We went off to college. He stayed behind.

That summer night with Ryan after my freshman year of college we were still too young get into a bar, so we bought beer with Ryan's fake ID, packed a cooler with ice, and parked beneath some trees in the lot behind my parents' house. We cranked the seats back so we could stretch our legs out, and spent the evening there, drinking one beer after the next as the city quieted and the lot's lights came alive in the dusk.

What did we talk about? How hot it was. High school, probably. And the woman at work that Ryan was sleeping with. He'd been trying to get his pilot's license, but a DUI put a stop to that, so he'd gotten a job in the warehouse at Walmart. He worked the forklift, and made more money in a day than Caesar and I did in a week from our internship stipends.

All night as we sat there with the windows down, the huge moon rising over the houses to the east, I avoided talking about college. Ryan was set to head to basic training on the first of September, a path that was almost unimaginable to me and Caesar. In our high school, it just wasn't what was done.

That sounds prim, and it is. But I say it to explain: the parents at our school—my own, Ben's, David's—were the hippies of the sixties who had ended up with money, or who had had it all along. The principal walked around with a Nalgene bottle connected to his belt by a carabiner. The auditorium looked like the concert hall of the Chicago Philharmonic, thanks to an anonymous donation by a parent who made certain everyone knew his identity. The motto over the school's front door said a school should be like a village common, an open community, but it proved to be a certain *kind* of community, with a certain politics that was permitted, and others shunned.

So I was scared that speaking to Ryan about college would seem like bragging, or that he might be envious, or feel we were rubbing something in. But now I wonder why. He liked his job. The warehouse jutted up to the edge of the Chicago River, and on his breaks he'd smoke on the riverbank. He could see downtown in the distance, and, along the river, the succession of old railroad bridges, locked in their raised positions like salutes. Crissy, the woman Ryan was sleeping with, lived on her own in Logan Square, and Ryan was over there more nights than not. He seemed happy, or something close to it.

When he asked me what I was doing for work, I was embarrassed to tell him. My first day at the congressman's office, during the staff meeting, the head of communications had looked in my direction and said there was only one thing I'd need to know: "The constituent is always right." When the phone on the conference table started ringing at the end of the meeting, she looked at me and said, "That's your cue! Do you remember what I told you?"

"Uh, the constituent's always right?" I asked, and everyone at the table burst out laughing.

I spent my mornings sorting mail, praying the phone wouldn't ring, thinking about what I'd get for lunch, and the lone cigarette that I'd have after. Each morning, my mother woke up early to make sure I had breakfast before I left. I looked at Ryan's life and then I looked at mine, seeing how childish it seemed in comparison.

The moon grew bigger as the night got later. The lights in the parking lot hummed in the heat, and the line of empty beer cans stretched all the way across the dashboard. Ryan was leaving in less than a week. Sitting there, the soon-ness of his departure suddenly flooded me. As a send-off present, I'd inscribed a book of war stories with a quote from Schopenhauer about human suffering I'd cribbed from the email signature of my freshman lit teacher. I'd wrapped the book in butcher paper and passed it to him proudly as the night wound down and he got ready to go home. I imagined him reading it in a barrack or something, at basic in San Diego or in the shade of a tent in a valley in Kandahar, leaning back in the hot afternoon, telling his friends about our stories from high school, idly thumbing through that book.

We tossed the cans in the alley dumpster. Ryan lit a cigarette. The moon was high and bright above us. He was getting ready to leave.

A little unsteady from the beer, I slapped hands with him, then leaned in to give him a hug. But as I did, he was beginning to turn away, saying something to Caesar, so as I grasped him, he was already leaning in another direction.

I sometimes find myself thinking about that moment. I think how, to someone else, I might've looked like a child trying to cling to a departing parent, and Ryan like the parent, trying to loose himself as he readied to depart.

I let go, laughing, and made a joke about being drunk to cover my embarrassment. I double-checked that the car was locked, and from the mouth of my parents' garage, I waved as they walked off down the alley, Caesar cracking up at something Ryan had just said.

A month or two later, reaching over to open the passenger's door, I looked down and found the book I'd given Ryan jammed beneath the seat, the front cover pinned back from where he'd left it wedged against the floor mat.

I laid my theory out to Rand. The Bush administration, in short, had employed Cold War–style fear-based tactics to gain support among Americans for an open-ended War on Terror.

It sounds almost lucid when I write it like that, but it took me a good seven minutes of talking, stuttering, apologizing, staring up into the air vents as I searched for words, hunting for a path through the ideas jumbled in my head, doubling back, smoothing my cardigan, finally arriving—kind of—at what I wanted to say.

"Well, so?" he said, when I finished. I was red-faced from talking and slightly out of breath. I was also freezing. The vents stationed above us kept raining down their flood of arctic air. I looked around, but nobody else appeared to be bothered.

"Well," I said. "The point is that everyone thinks of the war as being fought abroad. But what I'm saying is that there was just as much propaganda aimed toward Americans as there was at people in the Middle East."

"But doesn't any government have to sell a war to its public?"

"I guess," I said.

How was it possible that I'd not even considered that?

"But. Well." I was fumbling. "The point is that our government used the same kind of domestic propaganda tactics used in the Cold War. They want us to feel threatened, but they want the threat to be diffuse. They want us to be in support of the war, but they want life to feel like it's going on as normal."

"That's certainly an idea," he said. "Can you prove it?"

I laughed.

He didn't.

"I was hoping you might help me do that," I said.

Now he was laughing.

"Well," he said. "Outside this being just your opinion on the issue, I'm not sure what kind of evidence you're going to find. To be honest, I'm not entirely clear on why it matters. Like, what kind of evidence have you found? I mean documents, emails, whatever. Primary evidence."

"Can I—are you cold, by the way? Isn't it, like, freezing in here?" I said. "It's these vents. Do you think we could go outside?"

He looked at me a little perplexed, but shrugged as if to say, *Why not?*

While I swept the pile of papers and notes I'd laid out on the table into something manageable to carry, he threw away what remained of our drinks.

We got outside and walked toward his car. I sensed he was ready for this conversation to be ending.

"Look," he said. He leaned back against the car. The sun was in the center of the sky, bearing down on us like a spotlight. I tried to shift the mass of papers in my arms so I could pin them against my side with my right arm and use my left hand as a visor against the heat and the light.

"I think you have some interesting ideas, and could make a case for what you're saying. But I think you might get further if you asked a different question. I mean if you took an entirely different angle," he said, already opening the driver's side door. "I think you're working more in the realm of opinion right now, and I don't know how far that's going to get you."

He left me with his phone number, told me to let him know how things "shook out," then drove away.

I was supposed to call my mom when the interview ended, but instead I went back inside and ordered a sandwich, and just sat there for a while looking out the window. I wanted my mom to think the interview was so fruitful that it had gone on for a long time, so I bought another coffee, put my headphones in and put on music and let some time go by, drinking slowly, watching traffic pass, thinking how good it felt to be done with any kind of obligation for the week.

It's not that somewhere inside I wasn't worried over what Rand had said about my thesis. But any consequences seemed so distant that they didn't feel, in that moment, even real. It was almost the weekend. Casey, my college roommate, was already here. That was my connection to Spring Fling: Casey's girlfriend went to Palm Springs, and she'd told Casey to bring along whoever he wanted. Nina would arrive tomorrow. Spring Fling started on Saturday. If that wasn't an excuse for us to drink, I couldn't think what would be.

Nina's flight was scheduled to get in an hour after my mother's flight departed. My mom and I got to the airport early, and sat at a rickety round table at a grim "Café & Ristorante" opposite the baggage claim. That's what it called itself—a "Ristorante"—and somehow the foreign affectation only made the whole place more depressing.

Now that my mom was leaving, I was in a better mood. That was typical of me. As the end of a visit approached, I always began to feel guilty about how moody or reserved I'd been, and I'd try to make up for it in the last hours or minutes with a sunniness that must've seemed false and insincere.

My mother seemed sad. She stirred the cream around in her coffee and watched the people gathered at the baggage claim. They tapped on their phones, looking anxiously toward the curtain of cut rubber separating the outside portion of the carousel from the internal one. They were like people waiting for a train who keep peering up the empty track, as if their impatience might summon it.

My mom was quiet, so I talked to fill the silence. I told her about Nina and our plans for the weekend. I didn't mention

Casey or his girlfriend or the Spring Fling party; instead I said Nina and I were going camping. I asked about Dad and what their plans were for the summer, and how our two aging dogs were doing, and said I'd try to visit in July.

One thing I've always loved about my mom is how she responds to other people with openness—I could never imagine her putting anybody down. That's how I knew something was bothering her: her replies to me were short and terse, barely offering anything in return.

We sat there for a while. The pressurized entrance doors opened and closed. Wordless airy airport music played between PA announcements. A family in matching Disney shirts trudged past us, pushing metal carts piled with enough luggage to sink a small sailboat.

My mom opened her flip phone to check the time, then pushed her chair back from the table. I piled our cups into the paper bag my muffin had come in, and followed her toward security.

"Mom, you know I'm fine, right?" I said, before she got in line.

Nina arrived with just a backpack and a plastic glass full of something gold and bubbly, her chopped black hair pulled back in a ponytail.

"Guess what?" she said. "The flight attendant liked me." She was beaming, swirling the golden liquid in her glass. "So he gave me free champagne."

That was something I loved about Nina—how at ease she was in meeting the world, and how genuine her pleasure in something as small and kind as a glass of free champagne.

Nina was a freshman. She lived in the dorm bordering my own—my east window faced her west one, separated by only four or five feet. I found that out the first week of the school year when a rock knocked against my window. When I went to look, there was Nina before I knew her name, smoking out her dorm-room window, reaching a hand across the gap to say hello.

I've come to feel that I'm a person who receives their life rather than seeks it. I'm not proud of that fact, but that's how things started with Nina: the next evening, another pebble against the glass of my window, another cigarette I hadn't even asked for passed across the gap. She was from Cleveland, she said, "a painter," she told me, nodding at a heap of frames stacked in a corner of her room. When I said I had to go to dinner, she said she'd meet me downstairs. By the end of that first month, we were sitting cross-legged in our underwear on her bed's rumpled sheets, sharing a joint and sorting through a suitcase of old Polaroids, telling each other about our lives before we'd met.

We left the baggage claim and shared a cigarette under the terminal awning, then took the free shuttle that ran from the airport to the university campus. I'd reserved a spot for us on Casey's girlfriend's dorm-room floor for the two nights of Spring Fling. I'd felt guilty and nervous at the less than luxurious arrangement, but Nina wasn't bothered.

"It's not like we're here to sleep," she said.

It was a fair point. She'd agreed to take the trip down at the last minute, and I adored that about her too, how easygoing she was, whereas I was always fretting over every little thing. I remember being on the way to Ryan's once when Caesar got a phone call from his mother and had to go home. I froze. If Caesar left it meant it would just be me and Ryan until someone else came over. When Caesar got in a cab, I told him I was going on to Ryan's, but as soon as he pulled away, I walked to a bus stop and took the bus back home.

Isn't that an odd thing to do? I despised myself for it, but the truth was I was nervous to be on my own with Ryan. I think it had something to do with how much I admired him, or envied his confidence. In front of him I felt unformed, hazy in comparison, despite the way I'd cover it up by drinking and laughing and shouting like my friends did. But when he and I were alone, when his eyes fell on me, I worried he could see through that gauze to some kind of absence that I feared was at my center.

You'll laugh, but I once peed in my pants while standing in line to take an elevator over one hundred floors up to stand on the glass deck of Chicago's tallest building. It wasn't that I was scared of heights, it was that Ryan's father had taken us there, and as we got nearer to the front of the line, I worried he'd be angry if I asked to use the bathroom and made us leave our place.

I remember almost nothing from that day: not the city far below, not the curve of the earth they say you can see from that high up—only that somehow it was just the bottom of my pants the piss had darkened, everything below the knee, so I rolled them up till they looked like capris.

Ryan's dad kept asking me if that was a new style or something, like a look I was going for. He kept slapping my back and laughing. Driving home I put my sweater beneath me so his leather seats wouldn't get wet, and so no one would know.

Do you see what I mean? Every time someone mentions that famous quote from Jesus about the meek, it makes me think of me.

We'd barely dropped our bags in the dorm room before we were off for beers at a nearby bar. Casey bought us shots while his girlfriend, Molly, picked up pitchers for the table. Nina put Blondie on the jukebox, it was nine o'clock and then it was eleven, Casey insisted on shots for him and me with each round of drinks, and we called it a night at 1:00 AM to try and get a little sleep ahead of the parade in the morning.

It started early, Molly warned.

"We don't have to, but the freshmen start drinking at nine, so you probably won't get much sleep."

She wasn't kidding. We dragged the cushions off the couch as a makeshift mattress, Molly gave Nina her extra pillow, Nina lay down next to me, and when we woke the party was already going.

What woke us was the sound of Casey mixing drinks: ice grinding in a blender he'd rigged up on Molly's desk. Before I even opened my eyes I could feel my hangover. Blood thumped at my temples, and I kept my eyes closed to try to steady myself. The mornings after nights I drank too much, anxiety leapt on me as soon as it sensed that I was conscious. I was glad that Nina was there. The weight of her arm where it lay across my chest was calming, and she groaned at the sound of the blender steadily obliterating the ice.

"Sup, pups?" Casey said. "Time to wake up."

Casey was a statue: six one, blond hair, built like a boxer, perpetually in a loose-fit tank top that showed the mounds of his brown shoulders. We'd played club hockey together our freshman year (Pomona didn't have an official team), and we'd been friends since. His good moods were infectious. Nina untangled herself from me and looked over at him.

"Get dressed, you babies," Casey said. "The parade starts in two hours. We're having margaritas."

The desert heat was already smothering. I could tell by how hard the air conditioner was working, and how hot it was in spite of it. Molly came in with a towel wrapped around her. She was pulling a comb through her wet hair. Nina's face suddenly loomed over my own as I lay there, and she swept her black hair playfully across my face.

"Maaaar-gaaaaa-riiiii-taaas," she said, swaying her head to the rhythm of the syllables. I shut my eyes. I felt like if I moved too quickly I was going to be dizzy. I knew I needed to take it slow that day, to keep myself from drinking too much, or at least to pace myself enough to make it to the evening.

Forty-five minutes later, though, and we were on our second drink. This was typical of me. We stood out on the little balcony that opened off of Molly's room, laughing as she threw us different clothes to try on for the parade: a tie-dyed poncho; a yellow boa Casey draped around his shoulders; a candy-striped bodysuit Nina slipped on bra-less and wore with nothing more than a short pair of denim shorts.

That morning was so bright. Music came from Molly's speakers. Nina and Casey sang along the more they drank. I hadn't shaken the ache from my head, and could feel with each sip that I would be in bad shape when the effects caught up.

But the third drink replaced the hangover: halfway through, I felt something that felt almost good. I was standing against the sun-warmed railing, and Nina leaned against me. She leaned against me, my hand around her waist. She leaned back, and the way she placed her body against mine felt like a wish for us to be alone.

I know I said how bright the morning was, but what I mean is I felt hopeful. The music kept coming from the dorm room; the freshmen drinking on the lawn beneath us were clearly in far worse shape than we were; and there was just enough room on the little balcony to sit facing outward with our legs looped through the gaps in the railing, our feet dangling down into the air.

Near noon, Casey lit a cigarette, passed it to me, and lit one for himself. Why not? The smoke gathered in the motionless heat, we took long sips from the freezing beer, and Molly took pictures of each of us with a little Polaroid camera.

Here was a beauty of the morning: the midway point of the parade route was just one block east, and the thruway that led to it was visible from the balcony, so a steady stream of students passed along it on their way. Hearing our music, they'd look up, then we'd cheer down and raise our cups, then they'd raise theirs, day-drunk in the heat, zigzagging across the path, stumbling lovingly into the people they were with.

Nina was so young then. I sometimes forget that. Her long tan legs were deep brown from the California sun. Her paintings were her childhood—pale, almost faceless shapes lost among the grasses in a field; they were already getting so good.

When we finished our beers, we filled a backpack with more, then bounded down the dark dorm stairwell and out into the sunlight. People streamed along the parade route. We slipped in and were carried right along. Ahead of us, bright floats rolled down the center of the boulevard: a birthday cake, a purple unicorn, a rainbow bridge, a pirate ship. We walked behind them, crunching through the wake of beads and crushed cups.

It's strange. When I think back to that day, I can recall so much that happened in its broad strokes, but I remember so little of what was said.

We talked about the heat, I guess. We kept saying how good we were feeling. We shouted to the people hanging off the floats, hooting as they showered us with beads. Girls in sunglasses, tanned boys in backward hats—strangers to us but friends with Molly—emerged from the crowd and flung their arms around her. "This is Greta," "This is Jillian," "This is Mark." We said hello. We dug out beers to share from the bottom of our backpack. The parade kept moving. The names disappeared into the crowd.

Months later Nina received an email from Molly with scans of photos taken with the disposable camera Molly had been carrying around that day. In one, a stranger holds up her dog to the lens, its pink belly sprayed with spots of brown. In another, Casey climbs the flagpole on a frat house lawn, shirtless, a beer bulging from his back pocket. In another, I'm trailing behind Nina as we walk down a sidewalk in the shade, both of us turning back to look at the camera. Nina's wearing black leather boots and colored strands of Mardi Gras beads. I'm in an army-green crew-neck T-shirt, the skin beneath my eyes pale, my face bare beneath my shaved head.

What strikes me most about those pictures is how tired I look. There's something in my eyes in the photographs—something fragile, something worn out, something exhausted—that is incongruous with the scenes of celebration going on around me. I have money in my hands. I have my arm looped low around Nina's waist. I'm in a parking lot in a mob of people all facing one direction, but I'm looking over my shoulder in the other.

The parade ended where the "Half Mile" began—the long strip of bars, burger joints, smoothie shops, and taco stands that all the Palm Springs students flocked to. It was like a tributary finally arriving at its river: the people following the route of the parade finished their drinks or ditched them on the curb, and poured into the Half Mile's carless avenue, peeling off into one bar or another, every place along the strip showing the gold and blue of the school's colors, inviting the throng to descend.

I hadn't seen Casey before I left for Palm Springs, so he was seeing my shaved head for the first time, and he was having a field day with it.

"Private Katz!" he kept screaming, using my last name. "Semper fi, motherfucker!" He cracked up every time he said it. "Private Katz!" he laughed, his arm draped over my shoulders. "Someone buy this hero a beer!"

It was late afternoon. We were standing under the awning of a bar called Champs, finishing a cigarette, when someone started yelling at us.

"Your shirt, hey, your shirt!"

We looked around, then up into the sky. A skinny boy in a purple shirt was shouting down from the bar's third-story balcony. He was draped over the railing as though he wasn't scared of falling, though he should have been.

"Your shirt!"

He was pointing at Nina, though she wasn't wearing one. He meant the cape she'd draped around her shoulders. It belonged to Molly and said, *Elmhurst High* in cursive letters looped around a lion. He was trying to tell us he'd gone to school there too. The balcony he was standing on was as crowded with people as the parade floats. It overflowed with bodies, like fifty colored straws gripped in a fist. Loud music boomed. He gave up shouting and motioned for us to come up.

Nina and I split the rest of the cigarette, then she dug around in her purse for her fake ID. It wasn't a good one, but it usually worked, and we had a plan: Nina would be the third one in, behind Molly and Casey, who were both over twenty-one. We thought the bouncer would scrutinize Nina's less after seeing two IDs that were beyond suspicion.

We went to the back of the small line outside. For each person who left the bar the bouncer let one person in. Two people came out; two were let in. One person came out, followed—a few moments later—by another. He tripped over the threshold and stumbled away on the cement, calling out, "Kristie, I'm not drunk!"

Two more came out, and then it was our turn.

"You a group? The four of you?" the bouncer asked.

"Yessir," Casey said, handing over his ID.

The bouncer nodded him through, then looked at Molly's, then nodded Molly through.

Now it was Nina's turn. She reached in her back pocket to retrieve her ID, but it wasn't there.

She reached in the other one, but it wasn't there.

The bouncer tilted his head at her.

"Wait wait," she said, finally digging it out. She had lodged it between her hip and the elastic band of her shorts. He looked it over for a moment, sort of shook his head, then waved her through.

I handed the bouncer my ID, then was halfway through the door when his hand gripped my upper arm.

"Soldier," he said. I turned around, startled.

The bouncer had his left hand at his chest, pinching his shirt like he was trying to pick something off it.

He was trying to show me something on his lapel.

"See that?" he said.

I leaned forward, squinting.

"Fourteenth Air."

"Uh."

I was confused.

"Fourteenth Air?" he tried again.

I looked at him, unsure of what he meant. I just stared at him for a second, trying to piece it together.

"Desert Storm," he said. "Fourteenth Air."

And it clicked.

My shaved head. My army-green T-shirt. How Casey kept calling me "Private Katz" as we'd smoked outside the bar.

"Yo. Thank you for your service," the bouncer said, and instead of correcting him, I let him shake my hand.

I found Nina and Molly upstairs, crammed in on the bar's third floor. In the crowded room, people danced. Nina had her arms in a soft loop around Molly's neck, and they swayed together to the music. I pushed out to the balcony to find Casey, or a beer, and to get some air. I leaned on the balcony banister, looking down at the people passing on the evening street.

I never want to go back to Palm Springs. When I remember it, I think of the sadness of the desert light; the days rising and dying into the night; lying there sleepless as my mother slept on the bed beside me in the quiet motel; how I let that veteran shake my hand, then turned away.

It was years until I'd think of that moment and fully see the irony in it—that I had been mistaken for the soldier that Ryan really was or, worse, in never correcting the bouncer's perception, pretended that I was that soldier.

But as the years have passed, I've come to see it as another instance of what I said before: that the life I am living is not a life I've sought or made, but a life that I've received. So when I turn over that moment again, when the bouncer mistook me for a soldier, and shook my hand, I see another instance of allowing myself to be whoever someone thought I was, rather than admitting who I am.

I think that as I stood there looking down, I had some portent of what was to come. I sensed that I was in the beginnings of a pattern that would become my life. I'd arrived there hurt from the way that I'd been drinking, and I'd leave there hollowed, vulnerable and fearful, shaky in the tapering off after Spring Fling's binge. Nina and I would make our way to the back of the Greyhound bus. The cold air would pour down on us, thick with infection. The fear I'd felt on the bus ride there would return in full: nuclear weapons exploding deep beneath the earth. Radiation expanding like a galaxy in the silence of the ocean. My mother's hands more aged each time I saw her, the veins blue and raised against the spotted skin, how they'd lain on the table before her like two dead birds. The metal would scream as the driver eased the brakes. The engine would roar. Nina would look over at me. What was going to happen to us?

On the balcony, the light from the sinking sun spread evenly from the horizon. Everything was flooding in the glow. Nina stumbled onto the balcony with the boy in the purple *Elmhurst* shirt who'd called down to her an hour before. They came out laughing, as if he'd just finished telling her a story.

"Graham!"

Nina careened over, flushed from dancing, charged at me like a ram, burrowed her head in my chest, then fell back against the balcony railing, letting out a breath.

"I need a cigarette. Eliot!" she yelled. "Graham, this is Eliot, and he is a *lion*!" She was sputtering with laughter, pointing to the mascot on the boy's shirt.

She was drunk. We all were. They were both doubled over. She draped an arm over his shoulder as she laughed. They lit cigarettes, and again she draped her arm around him, as if they were old friends. I watched them, her small hand dangling on his chest, as if she thought I wouldn't mind.

And I didn't. But in that moment her assuming I didn't made me feel like I should. I looked around me. The world had quieted. The crowded bar was emptier. A girl and a boy slow-danced in the darkening room. It was evening.

Then Nina was in front of me thrusting something in my hands, but I was suddenly thinking of my parents. It was Saturday. At this hour they'd be together, making dinner. I thought of the blue pots simmering on the burners, my mother and my father fussing around the table, each of them silent in their thoughts, already thinking ahead into the quiet of the week. They were getting so old.

I looked down at the disposable camera Nina had pressed into my hands. She wanted a picture with her in her cape and the boy with his matching shirt. I took a few steps back and motioned them even closer to each other, but as I took the picture I kept one finger pressed tightly over the lens. The flash illuminated them—there on the balcony, twined in the cape, their eyes squinting with laughter—but the photo, when Molly finally developed the roll, would show only a sheet of black. I handed the camera back, sick at how small I was.

Back inside, we found Casey and Molly at the end of the bar, their half-finished beers pushed to the side. Molly was sprawled forward onto the bar's dark top, her chin resting on the back of her folded hands. Casey had somehow got his hands on a bag of hot dog buns. When he saw us, he tossed the package to Nina and started digging around in his pockets, searching for his bag of tobacco. Nina nudged her hip against Molly's, and Molly slid forward on the barstool, leaving enough room so Nina could perch there with her, the curve of Nina's back resting against Molly's as they looked off in opposite directions.

I watched Nina chew the stale bread, her eyes heavy but her face looped into a smile. Despite my sour mood, she'd already moved past it, or hadn't noticed. She seemed entirely given over to how she felt in that moment—still drunk, still soaked from the noise and color of the day. I envied that, how present she could be in where she was. She chewed slowly and stared into the air, her eyes lost inside her thoughts. I felt guilty before her. I wanted to make it up.

We made our way down the carpeted staircase and back out onto the street. Now it was night. The lamps came on. Voices called from one place to another. People trailed out of the bars. Cars started, doors slammed shut. Everyone was going home. Molly walked beside Casey as he wove back and forth, trying to roll his cigarette. They went ahead.

Then it was Nina and I side by side in the twilight of the thick heat, walking beneath the campus's lamplit lane and the early stars much farther above. I'd be leaving college soon. She still had three more years. I know I've said that. I've wondered why I keep remarking on it. Perhaps it's because I felt things wouldn't last, even then. Even then, I'd tell myself how young she was as a premade reason for why they couldn't.

We wandered down the dark street. She was singing a song from earlier in the day, entirely inside of what she was feeling. I was thinking of my own time in college: hockey all winter, "away" games in strange towns, sleeping in chain motels sprayed gradually gray by the highway's exhaust. I thought of summers back home, the shore of Lake Michigan, drinking with my friends, how I lay back and let my head hang over the edge of the dock, so the world for a moment was upside down. On the dark street, finally, I thought of Ryan, far away and growing still farther than I could even imagine. I leaned into Nina like a wall and pulled her close to me.

"I have to tell you a joke," I told her, but I'd meant to say "secret," so when she leaned her ear nearer to me, though I'd intended to say, for the first time, "I love you," what I said was something else.

Sophomore / Junior

Jana would come to forgive Ryan for what he did at the dance, though it would take a while. Two weeks after and she still refused to see him, so we ordered a pizza, and when his parents went to sleep, Ryan, Caesar, and I took a half inch from every single bottle of liquor in his dad's cabinet and combined it all in three empty Gatorade bottles, each one filled to the brim.

To this day I've never been sicker. I woke in the morning on his bathroom floor, face down in a cold pool of vomit. Even by eleven the next night, the numbers swam as I tried to do my math homework.

The spring grew warm. Jana still refused to speak to Ryan. We took refuge in his basement, playing video games late into the weekend nights.

When the school year ended, summer came, and we went our different ways. We returned to high school in the fall, giddy to be together again, almost shy with each other from our months apart.

Time had wrought its perpetual trick: my friends came back from summer the same, but different, each one taller, or their hair grown long, or wearing a new bracelet, with some new story, some new habit, some new secret, some new love.

Ben had shed his baby fat. David had spent July working for his cousin's moving company, until he'd lost his grip on an air conditioner. Its edge had crushed the big toe on his left foot, and he wore a boot all the way into November, like something an astronaut would wear in space. Caesar had gone to stay with family in San Antonio, and his summer was an entire novel: swimming holes, a bike accident in an empty construction site, a girl he'd met at the Lone Star Mall he texted constantly for the first month back, then never heard from again.

With Caesar in Texas, I'd gone back alone to the hockey camp in Michigan. In his absence, I felt on the outskirts in relation to the other boys. They seemed to make friends so quickly, to form so easily into little groups. Uncertain how to join them, how to become a part, I'd retreat to my dorm room as soon as I could. From the room's window, after dinner, I'd watch them on the campus common, gathered in their different clusters, talking, joking, slowly edging closer to the groups of girls from the theater camp, sitting on the far hill. It was a comfort to look away from those scenes and get lost in the world of whatever book I'd brought from our school's required summer reading list—*The Catcher in the Rye*, or *The Great Gatsby*, or *The Bluest Eye*.

Ryan shrugged when I asked and said his summer kind of sucked, but looking at him, all I could think was he'd somehow grown more handsome. He'd gone to Canada for summer league hockey but had come back early, and didn't tell us why. He said he'd spent the rest of the summer sitting at home, playing video games, getting yelled at by his mother, and lifting weights in the garage, in the space made newly vacant by the recent absence of his father's car (more on that to come). His shoulders had broadened; he looked like someone sunned from work—a mechanic, or those guys in bright vests on highway work crews, who don't much care, probably, but grow strong anyway simply because of what they do.

The bright spot, he said, was Jana. He'd called her all summer. She'd refused to see him. He'd shown up at her house with flowers he left with her mother. Jana agreed to dinner. He asked to get back together. She said she wasn't interested. He left letters in her mailbox. He gave her a ride to her dance class in the suburbs—first Tuesday, then Thursday, then Tuesday again, until eventually it became their routine. He told us how he'd sit for hours at a grim Krispy Kreme in Schaumburg while she practiced, then drive her back home. By the summer's end, they were back together.

"Well kind of," he said. "She says I'm on probation."

"What does that mean?" we asked.

"I'm not sure, but we're basically dating."

"It took her long enough," he added, but we could tell what it meant to him.

That was an odd year. It was 2002. We were sophomores. The wars that had started to dominate the headlines when we were freshmen, that had floated at the edges of our consciences as we shifted from skate to skate in ice rinks up and down the shore of the northern suburbs, now moved like a shadow more centrally into our lives.

All fall my parents held gatherings in our living room. Their friends from the sixties—hippies and musicians, protesters of Vietnam and nuclear weapons, most grown into an affluent middle age—converged on our home to plan rallies, trash Bush, or just get loaded with old friends on the armfuls of booze everyone who came through the door brought with them.

Upstairs, my friends and I carried on dumbed-down versions of the downstairs arguments. We'd sneak a bottle of whiskey from the kitchen and sit in my bedroom arguing about Bush and Cheney, moral war, the looming surveillance state, the Middle East. We'd been assigned an article in our civil liberties class called "The End of History?," and we kept throwing around the author's name—Fukuyama—like we knew what we were talking about. Out of all of us, only Ryan believed in the justness of the war, and by the bottom of the bottle he'd be in Caesar's face or Caesar would be in his, screaming something about nerve gas, stockpiles, Fukuyama, The End of History, both growing so nonsensical we'd all start laughing.

At that time, too, I began to notice that something was going on in Ryan's home. I still have no idea what the specifics were. We knew his father had a string of factories in Ohio. They made either bottles for hair products or plastic for toys—I feel certain it was one of those, but even then I wasn't sure which. Something had gone wrong in one of the factories, or something wasn't going well. His parents were fighting. His father drove off to Cleveland each weekend.

That's sort of the extent of what I knew. Coming down the stairs for dinner one night, I overheard my parents talking about it in the living room, but when I walked in they stopped. And though I never told this to anyone, one night at Ryan's, as I came into the kitchen, I stepped back into the shadows at the doorway, suddenly frozen by the sight of Ryan's mother, hunched over the kitchen counter, her shoulders, as she wept, shaking beneath her loose black shirt.

As Bush and Powell made the case for invading Iraq and my parents planned rallies in opposition, my friends and I continued on like we always did. We went to class. We drank at the steel yard. We went to hockey practice. We played video games in Ryan's basement in alarming chunks of time, descending at five on a Saturday afternoon and not emerging until five the next day.

One Friday in November Ryan dragged us to Jana's dance recital at a theater downtown. We bitched and moaned about going and stood in the cold parking lot for half an hour before going in, drinking gin and apple juice we'd poured into soda cups, but the performance was astonishing. We slumped into the theater in our hockey hoodies and baggy jeans, but everyone else was as put together as you would be for a funeral. I mean people were decked out: fancy dresses, high heels, suits and tuxedos, all the men in shiny leather shoes. That's what tipped me off to how good a dancer Jana really was: the theater was packed full, all three tiers of it. All those people had paid to come to see this company perform. We sat up a little straighter, ashamed to look as ruffled as we did.

Who knows what the performance was. There was an orchestra. The music was classical. The girls were almost astonishingly beautiful in their forms and in the way they moved. We snickered at the male dancers in their skin-tight pants that showed in outline everything underneath. But we were turned silent by the performance, both during and then for minutes afterward. When the lights came up, I followed Ryan and Caesar as they shuffled out of the aisle, but I was thinking of the circles of dancers, separating then flowing together then moving apart before returning in an intertwined form, the violinists plucking their strings in an even pizzicato, accompanying the dancers like the tick of a clock. I think we didn't speak because we knew whatever we said would've sounded insincere, or insignificant, or cheap in the face of what we'd seen.

By February, we'd swapped the steel yard for Friday nights in Devon's basement. It made sense—the basement was warm, Devon was Jana's best friend, her parents didn't care that we were down there drinking, and she and Caesar were now together—but in truth I missed those nights in the freezing steel yard, hiding from the wind in the shelter of the metal tubes, patting them when we left to say goodbye, as if they were inert metal animals, silent but kind.

I was always a little anxious arriving to or leaving Devon's. Her house was on the same block as Sam's mom's apartment, and I worried we might run into Sam. It wasn't that I didn't want to see her: even though we were no longer dating, I still cared for her, and for her life. I wanted her to be happy. But we hadn't spoken much since we'd broken up after that sad night at her older sister's party, when she'd cried against me in the bathroom, and I was always anxious I might bump into her when I was with Ryan, Jana, Devon, and Caesar. I knew it would hurt Sam to see us all together when she was no longer included, and I knew I'd want to reach my hand out to her, to ask her how she was, maybe even to invite her along; but I also knew I'd never have the courage to do that in front of all my friends.

After six or seven beers in Devon's basement, Devon would pair off with Caesar as Jana would with Ryan, and for the rest of us it meant the night was ending. I lived north of Devon's. David, Ben, and Neil all lived south. They'd start walking or head to Clark Street to catch the bus, and I'd wander through the neighborhood until I had to be back home.

It was winter in Chicago, so cold the world felt still. People not from there probably don't know this, but there's a small zoo in Lincoln Park, right there in the heart of the neighborhood, and most of those nights I'd end up there. The animal houses were locked, but the zoo itself was not, so you could wander on the long stone paths, listening to the sound of the owls calling from their perches behind the high mesh enclosures.

Even in the deepness of that cold, I liked my life in those moments. I liked thinking of myself as someone who'd walk through a zoo alone at night. I'd just seen this movie where the protagonist is in high school, though he seemed so much more adult than me. He wore handsome, expensive clothes. He lived in New York City. He kept a leather-bound diary where he wrote about things that were happening in his life—people he slept with; the hypocrisy of his parents; a new arrival at the school who he was curious about, and wanted to get to know. There was something in him—something that the diary signified—that I admired, or wanted to be. He was independent. He had an interior life. He provoked the curiosity of others because he had a certain disregard for what they thought. Even in the midst of a party, he might leave to be on his own.

My friends would've made too much fun of me if I had bought a journal on my own accord, but I'd had an excuse that fall when our English teacher assigned us all to buy one and keep a record of our days and thoughts, and then I kept doing it for years. I had tried to find a journal just like the one that belonged to the young man in the movie, and began to carry it with me everywhere, even there in the zoo, late at night. Whenever I ended up there, I'd stand looking south to downtown's crown of lights, then trudge down into the tunnel under the aquarium. The tunnel walls were made of glass that gave a view into the seal pool, on one side, and the tank of the sea lions on the other.

In my notebook, I'd record little things I noticed: a pair of shoes abandoned in front of a water fountain, as if the person drinking from it had vanished, leaving them behind; how the rounded walls of the aquarium tunnel made me recall those playground crawl tubes where, as kids, my sister and I would hide from our parents, stifling our laughter as they called our names.

At first, and for a long time, I didn't really feel like I had anything meaningful to say, so I'd imagine I was that handsome protagonist from the movie, and try to write what I thought he might've written. I wrote descriptions of my friends. I wrote about Lake Michigan. I wrote about how, in the daytime, children stood transfixed before the seal tank, their mouths open before the majesty of the animals. Down there in the tunnel, alone at night, peering through the glass wall into the black water of the pool was like staring into the heart of space. I'd get lost with my forehead pressed against it, looking into the depths, trying out different similes in an attempt to get the description right, the huge silver bodies of the animals suddenly appearing out of the dark like specters, like spaceships, like memories.

The wars were everywhere then—first Afghanistan and then, that March, Iraq—but they were everywhere abstractly: civics class, Model UN, the basket of peace pins by my parents' front door. Our junior year history teacher would show us *The Fog of War* but give us little context, expecting us to make the connections, but something was lost along the way: I would come away from it thinking McNamara was somehow good. I thought our teacher meant for us to sympathize with him.

Later on, when I was in college, in a conversation with my advisor, I would understand what I'd been meant to take away. I brought up that movie, and before I could say anything she jumped in excitedly, saying, "Exactly! I loved that: how the interviewer just let him talk, and he exposed himself as a war criminal."

But when I first saw the film in high school, I thought the lesson was that when we're in the middle of something, it is difficult to see the fullness and complexity of the broader picture. Half-asleep, with my head slumped on my desk, I found comfort in that idea. In the darkness of the room, I applied it to my life: that whatever was happening to me then, that no matter how confused or uncertain things seemed, I would be able to better understand them later on, from a different vantage, and that if there was something to forgive, I could be forgiven. I wasn't thinking of anything in particular then—what would happen with Ryan hadn't yet happened—it was just a sense that came over me in the warmth and the darkness of that room, cloaked from the bright afternoon outside, a reassuring notion that wrapped me inside it, like a blanket or a cloud that I was being carried in.

The wars were "bad," our parents said. That was the simplicity of the language they used. The election had been "stolen." Our troops abroad were an "occupying force." 9/11 or not, they said, Bush would've gone to war with Iraq. Standing at their kitchen counters, talking on their phones or chatting with a friend, our parents made a thousand variations of those same points. In the middle of their conversations, they'd look over at us as we tried to slip into the kitchen unnoticed for a snack or a glass of milk, expecting our assent.

And I did agree, I think. Ms. B had us reading Howard Zinn and Noam Chomsky. I took that class on civil liberties. I took one of my parents' handmade peace pins and pinned it to my backpack. One warm Thursday afternoon, I wore my father's suit to a Model UN session in which I presided over a mock trial on war crimes. Sunk into the couch on Monday nights, staring at the television, I watched footprints in the colors of our flag advance across a map of Iraq. The sandy background was replaced by the face of a reporter, who reported our troops' approximate locations. The only in-country video was night-vision footage from a camera fixed in place. It was like watching a live feed of the sea at night: mostly the screen glowed black, then green flashes would bloom in the distant background—which we had been told was Baghdad—but everything was soundless, like an aurora borealis.

Ryan never spoke about what was going on at home, or at least not to me. At times I felt it was his mother he was angry with. Our sophomore year, on certain weekends, he'd get picked up from school, then disappear with his father on trips to Ohio.

At other times, however, I felt it was his father he was angry with. We'd gather in Devon's basement, Ryan's backpack filled with cigars and whiskey I knew he'd stolen from his dad's study, because I'd seen them there.

Ryan had a credit card in his dad's name, and sometimes he'd use it to buy extravagant things: jeans and jackets he'd order online, whole wardrobes that must've rung up hundreds of dollars, a new PlayStation that showed up one afternoon when we were at his house. His dad was standing at the kitchen counter with a glass of scotch in his hand. Even so, Ryan opened the package right in front of him, sliding the black console from its crisp box, as if daring his dad to say something.

And then, for a while, Ryan simply stopped going home. It started on a weekend in November of our junior year. I saw him at a party on Saturday in the same clothes he'd been wearing at Devon's the night before. When I asked, he said he'd slept at Jana's and simply hadn't been back home. That night, he went home with Jana again. I didn't think anything of it when they showed up to school together on Monday, but then they showed up together on Tuesday, and again on Wednesday.

"My parents are out of town for the week," Ryan said at first, but he ended up staying at Jana's the entire month, and then for months to come.

But I'm getting ahead of myself. It was mid-March 2003, still our sophomore year: the city was frozen; everything was quiet, everyone inside. Steam billowed like factory smoke from downtown's grates, and the river was ice, twisting through the silent city like a snake through a house in which everyone is sleeping.

It was in that cold that the march against the war in Iraq took place. That rally became famous for its size and its ferocity. Despite the cold, ten thousand people gathered at Federal Plaza.

Afterward, unplanned, the protesters shut down Lake Shore Drive, the long road that runs along the lakefront, traveling the length of the city.

South to north, traffic stopped dead, and for a few hours the stern procession went forward like an army in formation, the great icescape of the lake forlorn and gray, stretching forever off the flank of the march. I think sometimes how strange that procession would've looked from above: ten thousand people, the downtown skyline at their back, the cracked expanse of ice to their right, the breadth of the marchers funneled in between the highway's stone sides, walking forward with no clear destination. There were shadow protests in cities all across the country—Portland, Seattle, San Francisco, DC—but later I'd study them, and see that none of them came close to the ferocity of Chicago.

Looking back, that makes sense to me. It was in the city's DNA, from the May Day Martyrs at Haymarket in 1886 to summer 1968, when the city erupted during the Democratic Convention as protesters gathered to show their rage against the Vietnam War. The Chicago Police, under the thumb of Daley, had been given the green light to batter the protesters into submission, by any means necessary. You've probably seen the pictures: Grant Park, Michigan Avenue, the mass of protesters, cops with billy clubs pouring from the backs of trucks, charging into the crowds of people like a wave overrunning the shore.

My parents and their friends had been among the protesters at the convention. They were seasoned. Some had been at Birmingham in '63, when Bull Connor turned the hoses on the marchers and went after them with German shepherds. My mother and father had been there. They'd traveled down to Alabama in April to register voters, and stayed for the next month. They'd marched that day in May and, in the aftermath of the violence, walked dazed and battered through downtown at dusk, searching for my mother's backpack. Around them, the boarded department stores stood placid in the silence, the black pavement littered with lost shoes and torn clothes.

My friends were split on whether to attend the protest against the war in Iraq. My parents would be there, and my whole civil liberties class, even the teacher, had voted to go, so I was going. Same with Ben and David, since they were in civil liberties too. Ryan said he would've happily gone just for the chance to skip class and troll the protesters, but he had too many demerits and couldn't afford another absence. Caesar looked up when I asked if he was coming, said, "It's fucking freezing outside," then went back to the game he was playing on his phone.

The first stop on the way to Federal Plaza was the footbridge at North Avenue that crosses over Lake Shore Drive. Before we'd left the school, we'd made a banner in class from a long roll of fabric and decorated it with peace signs and black hearts around block letters that read, DON'T ATTACK IRAQ. Our plan was to hang it from the bridge, so the cars passing beneath could see it. We turned onto Clark Street, walking two or three across and eight rows deep, trudging south as we made our way.

It was colder than I'd thought. It wasn't snowing at the moment, but three months of winter had left grim mounds of it in huge piles at the sidewalk's edge, and my feet got soaked, the snow and ice bleeding through my canvas sneakers. I was wearing a winter coat, but I kept it half unzipped, hoping someone might glimpse the rainbow of dancing bears walking over San Francisco printed on my T-shirt. It was an old Grateful Dead concert shirt I'd slipped that morning from my father's closet, and I wanted it to be noticed.

I'm embarrassed of that now, but at that time I believed the T-shirt gave me some kind of vague credential, or might signify to others a series of beliefs that I hoped they'd think I stood for. The way I felt then, the T-shirt signified more than the band. It meant kindness, weed, a lifestyle, peace. And I wanted people to think that I embodied those things.

When we reached North Avenue, we marched single file up the ramp to the footbridge. Up there, the cold was even sharper. The city rose in the distance, gray and foreboding. Ben and David kneeled down to unfurl the banner, then stood, and walked backward in opposite directions until the fabric grew taut. Cars streamed beneath us, plunging north on Lake Shore Drive. The lake spread out to the east like a tundra. A heavy wind blew in from the west, flexing and swelling the banner. Ben and David fought to lash it with plastic ties to the thin metal bars of the bridge. The wind was fierce. The lake's waves would have heaved, but they were frozen in place.

Jana and Ryan were closer than any couple I've ever known. I know that probably doesn't sound like much—"It was high school," "They were young," all those things older people like to say to be dismissive of young people's love. But as I sit here and write this all these years later, I've tried but can't come up with a couple that I've known since that I've considered closer.

What was their love made of? I see that I am really putting that question to myself, to try and understand why their story has become so important to me, what it was that made them close in the way I observed back then, and that I so closely studied. I keep coming back to the rupture of those years: Ryan beginning to isolate from his parents, and that he had chosen Jana as the one to confide in, and then to live with, whereas with the rest of us, he had chosen to keep his silence.

But there is also something else: they were two rare people who even at that age were totally and wholly themselves, whereas I've never felt I've known who I am. I've always envied that about them. I remember Ryan stumbling into a junior-year dance, stoned and frantic, but happy. He wore loafers so big they looked like balloon shoes on a circus clown, and he kept toppling over as he tried to do that move from Slavic folk dance in a circle around Jana—squatting, then jumping back up, kicking one leg out and then the other, raising his arms in little flourishes.

I watched Jana laugh that night as he danced around her, and it wasn't mean laughter either: her cheeks got red and she held a hand to her mouth to cover her smile. Even though he was stoned, she didn't get mad at him. The way I understood it, Ryan was making a fool of himself, but he was doing it for her, and so she was on his side. She clapped when the song ended and brushed confetti out of Ryan's hair. I still remember the gentleness and affection in that gesture. I would've done anything to be touched like that.

Ben and David finally got the banner fixed to the bridge. We were all shivering and stomping around to try to keep the cold away and the blood moving through us, but someone wanted a picture for the school newspaper, so we had to stand up there in the wind and the cold as a classmate jogged down the ramp and walked a little ways up the highway's embankment, until she was far enough away to get a shot of us. In the picture, we're all clustered around the banner, the letters skewed and the whole thing hanging at a crazy angle, but our message against the war is clearly visible to the passing traffic, the words surrounded by hand-drawn hearts in thick black marker.

We'd been too young to see it then, but the way we drank in high school left us dazed. Beer before liquor. Sophomore, then junior year. Waking in that pool of vomit on Ryan's bathroom floor.

I've worried that you might think that I'm embellishing, or taking pains to show the degree to which alcohol lived inside our lives. But I don't mean to do that at all. It's just simply—and it was startling for me to discover—that alcohol was always present. I didn't begin this story knowing that, but each time I reach down to more closely examine something that happened—a memory I have of Jana, or the events of a specific night in a specific year—I am haunted to find that alcohol was always with us, and shaded us—or shaded what happened—in ways that we were blind to at that time, and probably for a long time after.

Our sophomore year, like the following year and the year after that, we convened on Monday mornings at the metal benches by the lockers, one of us slumped with our head between our knees, still recovering from Saturday. If it wasn't Caesar, it was Ryan. If it wasn't Ryan, it was me. It was a relief to me to see them in the same state I was, though it kept me from seeing that our drinking wasn't normal. Most mornings, I woke in bed at 5:00 AM, a dread in my chest that kept me awake, though where it came from I wasn't able to say.

But it wouldn't be accurate to say that the relationship each of us had to alcohol was the same. Ben and Neil could drink on Fridays and Saturdays, then not think about drinking again until the following weekend. That would hold true for their lives in the future. Whereas Ryan, I know, even when we were sophomores, kept a bag of warm beers stashed in the bottom of his closet, and a flask he drank from through the week, then filled again with whatever liquor he could steal from his father's study. He was only fifteen.

Caesar and I existed somewhere in between. Caesar's parents were strict enough that it was too risky to keep liquor in his house, so he was restricted to drinking on weekends. Like Ryan, I always made sure to have access to a beer or two, stashing them in my closet, at the bottom of a box. Ben and Neil went on to have a mostly normal relationship to alcohol. Caesar and I didn't. But it was only Ryan who would have drinking upend his life—DUIs;

an inability to get through school; lost money, lost friends, lost months, lost jobs—though that chaos also saved him because it led him to get sober. By the time he got back from Afghanistan, he'd quit drinking altogether.

We trudged south. As we got nearer to downtown, the scale of the protest slowly became visible. I began to notice people with pins on their jackets, while others held placards or homemade signs with different slogans scrawled in marker or printed on their front: Bush's name in a splatter of blood; REGIME CHANGE BEGINS AT HOME; images of prisoners with their heads noosed in black hoods, their bare torsos bruised and split.

Now our small group from school was among the growing crowd of people marching to the plaza. Old Town's rich rows of expensive brick homes gave way to the Gold Coast's offices and mid-rise apartment buildings, a sea of seafoam-colored glass. The streets broadened. We walked on the sidewalk. Traffic roared past. Horns occasionally blazed out into the cold when the drivers saw the handmade signs that some of us were holding, whether in assent or admonishment we couldn't really know.

It was midafternoon. The traffic's gray exhaust rose from the gray asphalt into the gray sky. Street corners with car dealerships and fast-food chains glowed like gas stations in the early dark. As we walked deeper into downtown, nearing Federal Plaza, the buildings grew dark and taller, the crowd thickened around us, and there were wide blue barricades blocking cars from the streets, so we stepped from the sidewalk into the thickening stream of gathering people. The yellow stripes of lane markers passed beneath our feet, slick and shining in the freezing drizzle. Above us, in the bright windows of the long corridor of office buildings, people crowded at the windows to watch our procession.

It's odd to me how vividly I remember that detail: men gathered at the glass in groups of three or four, in their button-downs and khakis, their hands pushed inside their pockets. I'd see those same groupings when I got older—at office happy hours, at backyard barbecues and the edges of dance floors at so many weddings, men rocking back and forth on their heels, standing beside each other but looking outward toward something else, glancing sidelong at one another as they spoke.

And in a window in a corner building I remember for the thick red steel of its frame, a woman with black hair and a long dark skirt stood there on her own, like a figure in a Hopper painting, her arms crossed across her chest, hesitant, before she briefly lifted a hand in greeting as we passed.

There was a seed that existed in Ryan, mean and small. It wasn't the whole of him, but it was there. He was loyal, wild, frank, side-ache funny, but his humor could have a brutalness to it. Once, I watched him stuff a pillow beneath his shirt and sit down in the science hall beside Mary-Beth Carroll. She was a freshman. Everyone called her "Scary-Breath." It had something to do with an illness in her organs, but her stomach was oddly protruded from her body, and rounded, like a pregnant person fairly far along. Ryan sat there beside her without saying a word, pretending to be texting on his phone, until she looked up from what she was doing and noticed him, and the bulge of the pillow at his stomach mimicking her own.

One afternoon that winter of the march, sitting in his father's study, we'd crowded around as Ryan pressed *play* on a grainy video showing militants using a handsaw to cut the head off a kneeling prisoner. I turned away, but Ryan was fascinated. Caesar could stomach anything Ryan could, but the difference was in his reaction. After the video Caesar shook his head and said, "That's fucked up." Ryan watched it again.

When Ryan drank, whatever was contained in that seed became directed toward himself. He would approach a bottle of liquor with the methodical bluntness of someone committed to silencing something in himself, and, with a chilling meticulousness, walked the path to doing just that. When he got there, he could be startlingly cruel, even to those of us who loved him most, as if daring us to abandon him too. It was frightening to feel him turn on you. And it was frightening to see him turn on himself. He became, very quickly, someone who couldn't be helped, or who refused to be.

In the late winter of our junior year, at a party at Andrew Scaglioni's, a boy from the class above us leaned toward Jana as she was standing at the pool table, lining up a shot, nodded toward Ryan, and said, "When he's finished, can I get next?" Ryan came around the table, and then he was chest to chest with the kid, asking him what the fuck he'd meant.

We'd all heard the question. The boy had meant it harmlessly. At least I think he did, though it's true we'd all been watching Jana as intently as he'd been. It was difficult not to: her shirt lifting as she leaned forward, the band of her underwear peeking above the hips of her low-cut jeans, her red hair piling on the table.

"Chill the fuck out," the kid said to Ryan. "I was talking about pool."

But Ryan saw it differently, and it went exactly as you might imagine: drunk Ricky stumbled over to try and intervene, was bypassed by Ryan, and tumbled face down on the couch. The kid who'd spoken to Jana backed off from the get-go. Ryan spit in his face anyway.

By the end of it, it was the rest of us Ryan directed his rage against. Weren't we supposed to be his friends? Why hadn't we defended him? Didn't we give a shit about Jana? Where the fuck were we when we were supposed to have his back? He tripped down Armitage Avenue, calling us faggots as he stumbled backward toward a cab.

We walked east on Adams, chants from the protesters ricocheting off the glass and steel of the towering buildings. Trudging down the plowed streets, squinting into the biting wind, hunched against it, it felt as if the tall towers surrounding us hemmed us in, their dark mass crowding out the light. And then the buildings above us suddenly stopped, and the street opened to the gray width of Federal Plaza, the center of the protest, total madness, the courtyard crammed like a train car after a baseball game. People screamed through megaphones, others tried to climb the sculpture at the plaza's center, children swayed on their fathers' shoulders, the gray sky was suddenly visible and low, a square of it cut out from the crowd of surrounding buildings, like a mirror reflection of the plaza beneath it. We had arrived.

What happened was that the incident with the boy at the pool table didn't end with Ryan spitting in his face. Early our junior year, before he started living with Jana's family, a box had arrived at Ryan's house containing two black airsoft handguns, alarmingly lifelike steel replicas of real pistols, resting in a bed of wood shavings to protect their gleaming metal from being scratched in transit.

They were beautiful, black, and unexpectedly powerful—a shot at close range left a bruise like the bruise from a punch. They were frightening, honestly, and so heavy in the palm of your hand you could easily mistake them as real.

Jana detested them; she'd leave the house every time he brought them out.

"One of you is going to lose an eye," she'd say, stuffing her things in her purse. "And I sincerely hope it's Ryan, because this is his dumb hobby in the first place."

I have this memory of him—during one of those afternoons when Jana warned that he would lose an eye—approaching the back of the couch, where she sat, then wrapping his arms around her from behind.

"Will you still love me as a cyclops?" he asked.

"That's not a nice way to describe someone with one eye," she said. "But yes, I'd still love you, maybe even more. Then you'd never be able to shoot one of your friends, or a squirrel, or accidentally me, with one of those ever again."

"I'm not sure that's the soundest logic," he said, pointing out that having one eye was kind of like a built-in scope: he wouldn't even need to squint to shoot.

But as he walked Jana to the door that day, he closed one eye and looked at her and said, "I want to keep both so I can see you better," and she left, no longer truly mad at him.

I know that sounds hokey, but there was something in the way he said it—and he often said things like that—that was genuinely sweet, as if it were an earnest truth that he couched in humor, so there could be some plausible deniability whenever we ragged him for it later, which we inevitably would. But always in that moment of the thing said half in jest, what was said was heartfelt, and so Jana would put her arms around him no matter how miffed she was, and plant a kiss on his cheek, because she could feel the truth of it too.

What happened was he brought one to school. I mean a gun. The Monday after the incident with the kid at the pool table—he stashed it, apparently, in his gym locker. I didn't know that until I heard the crash of a body against the tinny metal gym lockers as I was changing after gym class, and by the time I'd fully pulled my shirt on, Ryan had the kid in a full-on choke hold. It was just me, Ryan, and Caesar in there with him. Ryan had eased the kid to his knees—his name was Roger but everyone called him Red, which seemed fitting in that moment, given the color of his face from the diminishing oxygen. Then, from the waistband of his pants, Ryan drew out the black handgun and pressed the muzzle of the barrel to Red's reddening temple.

I knew, immediately, that it was an airsoft gun, and that the damage it could do to Red was relatively minimal, but Red didn't know that.

"What did you want to say to Jana?" Ryan asked him.

Red could only choke out a gurgle in response.

"Think you're fucking funny?" Ryan asked him. "Is this?" he said, wrenching Red's head to the left so Red could see himself reflected in the locker room mirror, the gun pressed to his head.

He didn't have the time to answer, though, because just then the hinges of the locker room door squealed as someone entered.

Ryan flung the pellet gun from his hand. It hit the floor and skittered into the wall of lockers, then came to rest near my feet. I looked up to see the gym teacher, Mr. Owens, turning the corner, then instinctively flung the towel in my hands over the gun where it lay on the floor, as I realized what was just about to happen.

Ryan released Red from the choke hold as Owens came into view.

"Hey!" Owens barked. "Guys! Hey! Knock it off!"

Red's face was puffed like a puffer fish and so red it was like he'd just run a mile. He was on his hands and knees, sputtering and hacking as he tried to get his air back.

"This fucking—" He hacked and tried again. "This fucking. Psycho," Red sputtered. "Has a gun."

The air went dead at the word "gun."

Owens took a half step back, but before he could speak, Caesar did.

"Whoa whoa whoa whoa whoa," Caesar said. "No one has a gun."

Owens looked at us.

"What is going on here?" he said.

"No one has a gun," Caesar said again, raising his hands. "They were just fighting. Let's calm down."

I took a step nearer to where Owens stood, trying to quietly nudge, as I did, the towel covering the pellet gun deeper beneath the locker room bench.

"Search Ryan," Red managed to get out. "He has a gun. It was just against my fucking head."

"That's ridiculous," Ryan said. "I'm not carrying a fucking gun." He turned out his pockets and patted himself like he was being searched. "See?" he said. "Who carries a gun? Red's a fucking liar."

"Watch your language," Owens said. "And put your arms up," he added.

"Are you fucking kidding me?"

"Ryan, language."

"This is bullshit."

Ryan stood with his arms spread while Owens patted his ribs and chest, then his hips, feeling for a weapon. He did that with each of us.

"Okay," he said, finding nothing. "You're all going to Bradbury's office then. Let him sort it out. Let's go."

Bradbury was the principal. My mind was going a thousand miles an hour as Owens escorted us to the locker room door. He held it open, waiting for us to file out.

I was thinking hard. I knew they'd search the locker room while we were in the principal's office. If they did, they'd find the gun beneath the towel. It didn't matter if it was fake or not. Ryan would be expelled.

As soon as I stepped into the hallway I knew what to do.

"My shoes," I said, turning to Owens.

"What?" he asked.

"I don't have shoes on," I said, pointing down to my bare feet. "It's cold. Can I grab them from my locker?"

"Be quick," he said.

I sprinted back into the locker room, and took a glance back over my shoulder to see if Owens was watching me. He was still at the door, but he was keeping an eye on Ryan, Red, and Caesar in the hall, making sure they didn't start up again.

As I approached my locker I slid my bare foot beneath the bench, hooked it around the towel covering the gun, and swept it forward till the towel lay directly in front of my locker. I knelt, pretending to rummage for my shoes, my back shielding my hands as I slipped the towel off the gun and quickly shoved the gun into the waistband of my pants, pulling my sweater down as far as it would go.

"Katz, let's go!" yelled Owens.

I grabbed my shoes and made a show of hustling by slamming the locker and quickly slipping them on. I'd thought, for a second, to leave the gun there, or to try and quickly toss it in the wastebasket and hope it slipped down beneath the mountain of tissue and paper towels, but took a chance by hiding it on me. Having a gun was about as serious a thing as could happen in a school. They'd surely search the locker room inside out, but maybe wouldn't search us, I reasoned, since we'd been searched already. Either that, or I'd just made about the dumbest decision humanly possible.

I can remember very few times my heart pounded harder than it did that day, sitting before the principal, the gun tucked in my waistband, pressing against my thigh, how I kept pulling the hem of my sweater down, terrified it would ride up without me knowing and give the whole thing away. We swore up and down that Red was lying.

The principal didn't believe us, or at least asked us why he should. He knew, of course, that Caesar and I were Ryan's best friends.

"Why should I believe you?" he asked.

We just shrugged.

He said he was going to have the locker room searched. Ryan and Caesar glanced at each other, clearly anxious. They didn't know that the gun was on me, in the room we sat in, that the security team could search the locker room for years and not find anything.

As we sat there waiting for security to come back from scouring the locker room, I started to feel a greater calm. I pictured Mr. Owens overseeing the search, showing the security chief which locker belonged to each of us. We'd been forced to give them our locker codes, and I could picture them opening each one, ready to discover the gun and finding nothing, emptying out the wastebasket, coming up empty-handed, returning to the principal's office having to report that they hadn't found a single thing.

And that is more or less what happened. The principal thanked the gym teacher and the security team, and then turned back to us. We were off scot-free, I thought. I looked over at Ryan and Caesar. I started to get up.

"Not so quick," the principal said. "I want to hear from one more person."

Caesar looked at me and I looked at Caesar, then we both looked over at Ryan, who was looking blankly at the principal.

"Who?" Ryan asked.

"I think Jana might be able to tell us something," he said, and then the door to his office opened, and she was brought in.

Jesus. I hadn't even considered that possibility, but it immediately made sense in a way that turned my stomach: Ryan had been living with Jana's family for the past few months. The principal wouldn't ask Ryan's own parents about the guns, whether he possessed one, because there would've been no point: the school administrators knew by then—everyone did—that he was living with Jana and her parents. Jana was a straight-A student, a star-level dancer, admired by everyone, adored by her teachers, and could've gotten into almost any college in the country she wanted on academics alone, never mind her achievements as a ballerina. Everybody trusted her.

My heart was in my throat when she entered the room. She detested those guns. As she stood there, she wouldn't even look at Ryan. She just nodded in greeting to the principal, and stood beside the chairs we sat in, waiting for him to speak.

"Take a seat, Jana," he said. "Take a seat."

He settled back into his leather desk chair, then shot up as he realized there wasn't a free chair in the room for Jana.

"Oh right, right," he said. "Ah, here, right, um, yes, I guess, yes, just take mine," and began to roll his chair toward her, then noticed the spray of crumbs from his lunch scattered across its seat, and leaned down awkwardly over the chair's high back to try to brush them off, nearly folding himself in half.

Jana had that effect on people. She was so pleasant in her look and affect that you instantly wanted to please her, and often looked like a fool in your hurry to do so.

The chair situation got sorted. Then, without a place to sit, the principal, his face a little flushed from embarrassment, stood behind his desk with his arms crossed, looking down at us.

"I'm sorry to pull you out of class," he said to Jana. "But a very serious accusation was made today, and I want to ask your help."

"Of course," Jana said. "Ask anything. I hope I can help."

"Do you know what happened?" Principal Bradbury asked.

Jana nodded. "I think so, at least in broad strokes. Mr. Owens said there was a fight between Ryan and Red. But I don't know much more than that."

Principal Bradbury nodded and made a little sound of affirmation.

"That's good, actually. That'll be more helpful." He stepped to his right, nearer toward Jana. "What I want to ask you is . . ." He paused. "Let me restart," he said. "Jana, I know, from conversations with your parents, that Ryan has been staying with your family these last few months. I know that there's a lot going on for him. I know you care for him. I know your family does. And what I'm going to ask you is in the interest of everyone's safety: his, yours, your family's, your classmates. What I want to know, Jana, is if you know anything about a, um, this is odd to say, a gun? Does Ryan own a gun? There wasn't just a fight. Red says that Ryan came to school with a gun, and that he pulled it on him. That's a serious accusation, obviously. Are you aware of a gun that Ryan might have?"

I looked over at Jana. Her hands were resting together in her lap, and she was looking down at them, her head nodding slightly in the silence that followed the principal's question, the clock ticking on the plain gray wall.

Still she wouldn't look at Ryan.

"Jana?" the principal asked.

She lifted her eyes to meet his.

"Yes," she said.

My heart raced harder. I looked over at Ryan, who was looking at Jana, but despite what she'd said, his face showed no reaction.

"Yes?" Principal Bradbury asked. "Meaning yes, you are aware of Ryan having a gun?"

"Yes," she said, and my mind went white.

The clock ticked, Principal Bradbury straightened to his full height, took a deep breath, then opened his mouth to speak.

But before he could, Jana continued: "And I also know that Red isn't telling you the truth."

Ryan, Caesar, and I—like a cartoon of men at a bar swiveling to watch as someone beautiful enters the room—suddenly and all at once swung our heads in Jana's direction.

"Ah," the principal said. "How is that exactly? You just admitted to me that Ryan possesses a gun."

"Possessed," Jana corrected.

"Excuse me?" Principal Bradbury asked.

"I said he possessed a gun, not possesses. And not exactly a gun, Mr. Bradbury, but a pellet gun, like a BB gun, basically, you know?"

"What are you saying?"

"I'm saying that Red is lying. I don't like guns," Jana explained, "fake or not, and Ryan hasn't had one for four months. Previously he had two pellet guns, but before I agreed that he could move in with us, I made him throw them out. I stood there as he did it. I watched him do it. That was the deal. Whatever else happened with Red, I don't believe Ryan pulled anything on him. Also, where is this gun you're talking about?" she asked quizzically. "Did you find one? May I see it?"

And the principal had to admit that they had not, that there wasn't one, that it had just been Red's word against Ryan's and that there was nothing, in the end, to back it up. We were free to go. Jana's story was pure invention—she detested the guns, but she had never made Ryan throw them out—but because of her lie on his behalf, we were free to go, and we went.

Back in the plaza, at the heart of the protest that cold March day, a trio of drummers beat time at the center of the swell of people—three quick beats that marked a call. The crowd, in turn, chanted in response:

Beat—Beat—Beat
DON'T ATTACK IRAQ!
Beat—Beat—Beat
BRING OUR SOLDIERS HOME!

Even amid that mass, I was embarrassed by the sound of my chanting voice. The people around me shouted with such purity of rage, such absence of self-consciousness. But when I raised my voice to add it to theirs, something didn't feel right, or I felt somehow like I was doing it wrong. Their shouts came from them with surety. My own sounded false and uncertain.

A black stage rose at the north end of the plaza. Its trimming rippled in the afternoon wind. An empty lectern waited at its center. On either side of it, facing outward, toward the crowd, stood a line of military mothers. Each one held an oversized picture of their dead son or daughter. As we'd entered the plaza, someone had thrust a sign into my hands, and now I looked down to really examine it: it showed a rainbow blazing over an image of, for some reason, Martin Luther King Jr.

Somewhere in the crowd were my mother and my father. When they'd returned from Birmingham in '63, they'd started organizing in Chicago against police brutality, and for better housing for the poor. I picture them in that frigid winter of '64, on folding chairs on hardwood floors, in the cold gathering halls of Chicago's Uptown neighborhood, people gathered round, talking, smoking, laughing, making plans, half of them with little children bouncing on their laps.

My parents were part of the wave of young leftists inspired by the Black-led organizations who were bringing the Civil Rights

Movement to the north. The work my parents would do the rest of their lives started in those rooms in Uptown. There was just a single couch in the office in the back, and a motto on one of the walls that said, "No Rest Until We Win," so the bargain became that anyone who wanted to sit down on the couch to rest had to play something on the guitar while they did; so—as my mother told it—as people worked, day or night, there was always music.

Searching that crowd for my parents, looking at the line of mothers up on stage, I was beginning to understand that they had earned what they stood for. They had fought and they had suffered. They had suffered because of their own losses, or because of injustices experienced firsthand, or injustices that they had witnessed.

I saw a movie once where a woman's husband dies too young, and she's left to raise the children on her own. In the middle of the night, her son is woken by a sound coming from somewhere in the house. He walks through the dark rooms, following that terrible sound, and through the gap in the bathroom door watches his mother pacing back and forth, clawing at her face, every few moments letting out a howl of pain so searing I knew I'd never watch that film again.

There was something in that line of mothers, in the bare fact of their grief, and how clear it was what the stakes were for them, that made me ashamed of myself. They had lost their sons to war. The sign I clutched in my hands seemed hollow in comparison, unearned, insincere. In that packed plaza, I ached for someone to get on stage and take the microphone. I ached for some kind of proceeding to begin. I ached for something outside me to quiet my own false voice. I wanted a reason to fall silent and listen, rather than struggle to be a part.

One Friday late in May my junior year, when all my friends were on their way to Caesar's, I lied and told them I had to help my dad with something and would meet up with them later. But instead of going home, I took the long path through the park to Diversey Harbor, then passed under the bridge of Lake Shore Drive, out to the little amphitheater of stone that overlooked the harbor inlet and the endless blue width of the lake itself.

That day, I sat on the stone ledge and just thought things over for a while. I think I felt I wanted to remove myself from everything that was expected of me. I think I was trying—though it would've been impossible then—to step outside the fog for a minute and see the past two years from farther away: the video of the beheading; the incident at school with the gun; the march to Federal Plaza; why I'd felt so out of place.

I thought about what I'd done for Ryan by hiding the gun. Did he love me for what I did? Maybe. He was certainly appreciative. He threw his arm around me and called me a mensch, and kept on doing so for months. But, if anything, the result of that day was that his and Jana's love was even more fully cemented, the two of them even more inseparably connected, because despite what I'd done to help him, what she had done was greater.

I thought about how it was—or why it was—that Jana loved Ryan. He farted in class. He'd sneak up behind her after gym, his shirt soaked with sweat, and catch her in a bear hug. He'd go off with us and not return her calls. He would lie to her about where he was. He'd drink too much, and become cruel. For a long time, I thought to show someone something in yourself that you weren't proud of was a bad thing. I thought you were meant to hide it, and that if you did, it might come to not exist.

Nina once told me that she never felt she truly knew me. She said there was something remote in me, something she felt she couldn't reach. It was only when I was drinking heavily, she said, and how I acted toward her then, that she believed I really loved her. I write those words and almost cannot breathe at how sad that seems.

Much later in my life, I'd wake one morning thinking about movies, and if they'd given me a mistaken understanding about how love between two people forms. Love in movies seems like something that happens to you, rather than something that you build with someone else. I saw one once where two strangers sit beside each other on a cross-country bus. He spills his suitcase in her lap. She falls asleep against his shoulder. They make small remarks about the passing landscape, and by the time they reach Cleveland, you're supposed to believe that it would be impossible for them to go back to their other partners, their other cities, their other lives.

Whatever love is, the movie suggested that it happens in an instant, and that its spell will be silent and mutually acknowledged. So I turned the movie off believing that's how love works, and that when it arrived in my life, it would bloom from a similar lack of volition.

Those films, I came to see, didn't teach me anything about vulnerability. They didn't teach me what seemed to come so effortlessly to Ryan: that to be loved, you have to risk something. That to be loved, you have to give someone else the chance to see you as you are. To be loved, you have to admit that you desire another person. In the face of the possibility that they might not say it in return, you have to admit that you need them.

Ryan, I see now, couldn't help but be entirely himself. Back then, I thought that Jana loved him in spite of that. Now I see that she loved him because of it. To appease, to please—I thought that that was what would make a person love me: to reflect back what I thought they wanted, or who I thought they wanted me to be.

And I changed who I was to accommodate. Or perhaps that is simply who I am—a reflection—or at least that is the person I've become.

Senior

In the room in which I write this are all these strange ephemera from my "Long Twentieth Century": the Martin Luther King Jr. sign I was handed at the protest; the folded American flag that Ryan gave to me when he enlisted; the poncho from that day with Nina in Palm Springs.

"The Long Century." I first heard that phrase my first autumn of graduate school, trying to extract myself from a circle of young bearded men who all seemed to idealize Marx, each of them taking turns talking about the "long centuries" of their particular area of academic interest. They kept using that term, like, "The Sugar Trade and the Long Eighteenth Century," or, "I am of course referring to the Long Nineteenth Century." I know what it means now, but at the time I thought, *Isn't every century long?*

To tell the truth, I wasn't very happy in my life. I had stayed in Southern California after college, working as the receptionist at a small nonprofit in Los Angeles while I applied to a grad program in public policy at UCLA, which I began the following year. Ryan was still in Afghanistan. Caesar had left to teach English in China, and it would be a long time before he ever came back. Ben and David were living on the East Coast, making their way, deeper each year, into comfortable lives. Nina and I had split (that was my decision), but she was close by, finishing college.

I looked around and felt confused. I was exactly where I'd told myself I wanted to be—in graduate school, on my way to a master's degree—but something wasn't right. I dragged myself to class, dozed on a slab of stone in the courtyard during breaks, finished a six-pack on my own most evenings, then did it all again. One night, as I was leaving a bar, a man grabbed my hand and asked if I needed "tickets" for the show. By "tickets," he meant cocaine. I said yes. There were repercussions.

I lost $400 on a street corner in Los Feliz. I fell asleep at midnight in somebody's flower bed, but when I woke I was mid-stride, inexplicably, and it was morning: I came to in the middle of the street, walking through East LA, missing my shoes but with my phone and my keys still miraculously inside my pockets. I flagged the first cab I saw and when I made it home, I literally got down on my knees to thank God I was alive, then went to sleep.

The summer before Ryan left for basic, I met a friend of his who told Ryan and me a story that I've never been able to forget. His friend was older—in his early thirties, I guessed. They'd met while taking classes at the community college. They'd become friends, and liked to drink together.

Ryan's friend framed the story as something funny that had happened after a bad night of drinking, though I wonder if he shared it because he couldn't stop thinking about it, and because, perhaps, it haunted him, as it has, in time, come to haunt me.

The story went like this: he had been on a bender—booze, cocaine, the nights bleeding into the days. Somewhere in the middle of it, he remembered that his dealer had once told him about a woman he knew who often "needed help with rent." The implication, Ryan's friend understood, was that for the right amount of money, the woman would do whatever he wanted. He had dialed her number, and an hour later she texted to say that she was waiting downstairs. And this is where Ryan's friend insisted the story was funny: the woman, when she arrived at his door, was visibly pregnant.

"Isn't that funny?" he asked us as he told the story.

"Isn't that funny?" and tried to make it so, telling us how out of breath she was by the time they reached his bedroom; how badly she needed to pee as soon as she started undressing; how she still had a small wet bit of toilet paper clinging between her legs as she lay on the bed, her eyes half-closed, as if she were trying to sleep.

I share that story with you here because I saw in it, during my time in LA, something I feared in myself: the fatigue he admitted to feeling in the days after that happened; sleeping to try and smother his self-disgust; a suspicion that my decisions were beginning to grow out of my control, or that they could lead to something irreversible or that I'd never be able to forget.

I have thought, as I imagine you must too, that he should've simply helped her: given her the money without asking for something in return; made her something warm to drink; called for a cab to take her home. I've always wanted to think of myself as someone who would do the noble thing. But that year in Los Angeles, I thought of Ryan's friend's story, and I wondered.

From here, I can see just how unhappy I'd become, but at that time, I fanned out the facts before me like a deck of cards, and they never added up: I had friends I loved, and who loved me in return. I was in the exact grad program I'd dreamed of being accepted to when I was still in college. I had a nice place to live, decent health, parents who supported me, a safety net of family and resources that I saw, as I grew older, was not as common as I'd thought. I looked at the facts and there was nothing really wrong. But as when I'd been in high school, I felt this great dread I kept secret from everyone else. I couldn't sleep. My gums ached and bled when I brushed my teeth. I looked around and tried to pinpoint a cause for my suffering, but found nothing. I accused myself. I drank to take me away from myself. Then I drank as a remedy for drinking's effects. My life became a wheel.

Our senior year of high school, Jana's audition for the dance program at Oklahoma City was set for the first Saturday in November. The school's recruiter was coming to Chicago to watch her dance, and we'd been driving Jana nuts. We kept jokingly calling it the "Juilliard audition," because I'd once seen a movie where the teenage girl is a really good dancer, and that's the school she dreams of getting into.

Jana rolled her eyes each time we said it, then explained for the hundredth time that Oklahoma City actually had the better program and was the harder school to get into, though nobody outside the dance world knew that. There was an instructor there whose choreography she really loved, and who she wanted to study with. The woman had been a dancer herself, and one night in Ryan's basement, when we were all in good spirits, Jana pulled up an old video of the woman dancing in Munich with the Bavarian State Ballet.

None of us could come close to appreciating what we were seeing in the way that Jana could, but I've never forgotten that video: the golden bridge in the background, the dancers collapsed on the stage like blossoms crushed on pavement—and how the dancer Jana liked so much danced alone on the bridge above them, the strings in the orchestra stripped back to their barest notes, marking time in the quiet as the dancer fluttered like something caught in the wind, from one side of the bridge to the other.

Much later I watched a movie where a pianist picks up a score he's never seen before, and as he looks over the notes for the first time, he begins to hum the music out loud. That notion astounded me—that where I see just black scratches on a white page, someone else looks at them and begins to hear actual music in their ears—how beautiful that must be. That's what it must've been like for Jana showing us that video: what she observed was so much deeper than what we saw, our beers sweating in our hands as we peered over her shoulder. But I remember it, and I think that says something about its power: I couldn't read the notes, so to speak, but there was something coming through that I could hear.

When I think about what happened—when I try to deflect blame from myself, or search for the starting point of what would occur, I keep coming back to the strangeness of the warm weather, and how late it stayed into the fall. It was our senior year. We all kept waiting for the cold to come, but even by Halloween it was warm enough that Principal Bradbury agreed to take a turn in the dunk tank during the annual October Fair.

And the warm weather held. We were still wearing T-shirts the first weekend of November. Neil's grandparents had already left for Florida, and their house in Michigan, on the shore of the lake, was just sitting there vacant. We made plans to go up there the weekend of Jana's audition. Ryan put up an argument, but we eventually got him to agree: we'd drive up Friday after school, spend the night by the beach, and he could catch the afternoon train back to the city on Saturday while the rest of us stayed till Sunday. Jana's audition was Saturday at 7:00 PM. He'd be back in plenty of time.

Jana was not happy. Ryan didn't say anything, but he didn't need to. The whole ride to Michigan he sat slumped in the front passenger's seat, his feet braced against the dashboard, his head bent between his knees as he texted on his phone.

"Jesus Christ," he'd mutter from time to time, banging his head on the headrest in frustration at something Jana had texted, desperate for her not to be mad at him, to see things from his perspective. I felt bad for him. Not because he was arguing with Jana, but because we'd convinced him to come, and so Jana being mad at him really fell on us.

We had a routine around our drives to Michigan. There was an ancient McDonald's just past the toll booths when you exit Chicago to the south. The wide line of booths loomed like the city's final gate. Even if you weren't traveling far, you felt like you were going on a journey. But as soon as you passed through it, you were immediately greeted by the bright yellow of the golden arches, planted squarely in the middle of the highway, dividing the northbound lanes from the southbound ones.

We pulled over every time, loading up on a bag of dollar cheeseburgers and shovelfuls of fries. We'd each get a Mountain Dew and, except for whoever was driving, would fill it half with gin, so as we drove farther north, as the city receded behind us, we felt a growing brightness, the desolation and municipal grimness of Gary, Indiana, giving way to something that looked much more like the true Midwest that surrounded us: billboards with torn ads for long-gone fireworks stores; farms, industrial sprinklers, silos; low acres of fields and greenery stretching in every direction, made brighter by the gin.

Neil spent the drive arguing to Ryan that since Jana was already mad at him, there was nothing he could do about that. He'd be back in the city tomorrow, Neil reasoned, so he should at least take advantage of being with us tonight. And he did.

All night we drank tequila and Dr Pepper. Moonlight shined on the ripples of the lake. We could see it from the screened-in porch, the soft waves breaking gently on the shore, frothing on the shoreline's rocks, retreating back out. The porch leaned out from the house, extending into the space of the bluff overlooking the lake, so if you turned out all the lights, it was like sitting in the night itself, the shapes of the tall trees slowly emerging through the darkness.

Beer in the cooler, tequila on the table. I know I said it before, but I've never met anyone who would drink so single-mindedly and destructively as Ryan did. He poured one shot, drank it, skipped the chaser, then poured another. After three or four, Caesar reached his hand out to stop him, but Ryan poured a fifth, and then a sixth.

All this happened in the course of just a few minutes; he did it as quickly as possible so as to forego the chance to reconsider, or think too much about the repercussions, the alcohol inside him but its effects still on their way. When they finally caught up, the night went on, vivid then less so. We played a game called Land Mines where you spin a quarter on the table and have to chug a beer for the duration of the quarter's spin. A bottle broke on the floor in one room, so we continued drinking in another. Ryan unearthed a tape measure from a wicker basket in the corner, and all night kept measuring the distance between himself and the rest of us as we sat around the table.

"Look how far you are from me!" he kept repeating.

"Look how far from me!" as he pointed it at one of us and then another, the unfurled tongue of tape drooping at its end as he reached it toward us.

And then it was so strange: we were banging on the foldout table, then the foldout table was toppled on its side. Caesar was leaping from chair to couch to ottoman, pretending the floor was lava; Neil was wrapping a silk scarf around his head like a mummy, the yawn of his mouth visible through the fabric as he laughed; we were in the kitchen, then we were on the lawn; we were running toward the road; we were running back; time was slowing; time was flying; and when I snapped back to a steadier present, we were all at the bottom of the long staircase descending from the bluff to the lake, staggering toward the black water, and I remember how cold the sand felt on my feet, and how huge the dome of stars above me when I looked up.

In the morning, the rest of us were already sitting around the glass table on the screened-in porch when Ryan finally woke up and joined us. Caesar had made Bloody Marys; the smell of bacon was coming from the oven. We were hungover, but the vodka in our drinks softened how washed-out we felt. By the time we finished our second, we were buzzed enough that we were able not to think about how terrible we'd feel by the time our hangovers finally caught up.

"Fuck me," Ryan said as he leaned in the doorway, shading his eyes against the morning's light. "I need to figure out what time I'm leaving, then give me one of those," he said, pointing at what we were drinking.

Caesar looked Ryan up and down, raising an eyebrow. Ryan was in his underwear and a faded T-shirt, worn away by sleep and time. He rubbed his knuckles into his groggy eyes.

"What?" Ryan said, smoothing a lick of hair that popped back up right after.

"You're missing a sock, guy," Caesar said, pointing down to one of Ryan's blunt bare feet.

Ryan looked down, said "huh," and wiggled his toes. "I need to figure out what time my train is."

"You need a drink," Caesar said. "And the schedule for the train is on the fridge," he added, nodding toward the kitchen. Ryan turned and stumbled in that direction. Neil and I looked down into our drinks, avoiding each other's eyes as Caesar avoided ours, knowing otherwise we'd burst into laughter and give up the whole thing.

It was turning out to be a beautiful morning. The lake was the same light blue as the midmorning sky. The low waves rolled in, calm and constant, breaking on the shore. From up on the bluff, shaking off our hangovers, each of us became slowly attuned to it: the crash and wash of the water coming and receding, the shimmer of the trees' leaves as they were ruffled by the blowing wind, the birds calling back and forth through the high clear air. It quieted us for a moment. We let our breathing slow, feeling the calmness of time in the quiet around us.

We were each reached in some way by that momentary peacefulness. Caesar leaped up and clapped his hands and got to work on another round of Bloody Marys. Neil hooked up his phone to the speakers to put on music. Ryan did push-ups in the corner. Ben lay on the floor in a pane of sunlight, his eyes closed and his hands crossed over his chest. And I took a minute to simply sit, sunk back on the cushion of the big wicker chair, facing out toward the woods separating the house from the lake.

I sat there looking out at the forest, the trees, the spaces between them where the lake and sky glinted through. I tried to be still; I wanted to capture it. I wanted to try to hold, for a moment, that peacefulness. I wanted to keep, before time kept carrying us forward, that whole picture, that whole morning, clearly in my mind.

We put ice in a cooler and packed it with beer and bottled water. We slung beach towels around our necks, kicked off our sneakers on the lawn, and trailed one another down the staircase to the shore.

On a clear day, if you're looking closely, you can look southwest from the beach and see all the way across Lake Michigan to downtown Chicago, its tallest towers like two silver scratches on the far horizon. We set up the beach chairs in a semicircle around the remnants of the fire from the night before. Neil put on music, we each sipped slowly from our cans of freezing beer, Ben lay on his stomach on a blanket, looking out at the water. That late in the year, the beach was usually empty, but the warm weather had brought people from the city to their cottages and summer houses. They strolled past in the surf as the day warmed and the sun rose higher, sometimes lifting a hand in greeting as they passed.

It was warm enough to swim. We waded in, wincing as the waves broke first against our knees, then against our thighs, then against our groins, then against our stomachs as we trudged farther out. Finally we did what we knew all along we'd have to do, and just dove in, surfacing breathless and gasping at the cold, arching onto our backs, kicking out into the deeper water, spreading our arms to steady ourselves as we floated, staring up into the wide blue sky.

What I liked best was finding the sandbar, and standing, and turning back to look at the shore from which we'd started. It stretched out for miles and miles, disappearing in each direction like the coast of an ocean. With the sun shining and the water dripping from my hair down into my eyes, everything took on a different hue, like the haze of a Polaroid, or the soft yellow shimmer from a tree strung with lights on Christmas.

The bluffs were flooded with trees—green—and still so full of leaves they seemed to breathe each time the wind moved. The other guys swam off to my right and waded closer to the shore, splashing and shouting and diving down just to resurface behind one another, and one would wrap his arms around the other's chest and pull him under.

That was my favorite part of the morning—being with them but separate, trying again—as I'd tried earlier on the porch—to slow myself for a moment until I could simply be where I was. And for a moment I believe it worked—up to my knees in the sparkling blue, water dripping in my eyes, the deep wall of green breathing on the shore—and then I remember saying, *thank you* under my breath, *thank you, thank you,* to God or space or whatever's up there, just *thank you,* before plunging back in and swimming over to join my friends.

It was late by the time we came back to shore. Later than we'd expected. Ryan had just fallen back into his beach chair and opened another beer when he tugged his watch from the sand by its strap and said, "Oh shit, I need to get going." Jana's audition.

"Noooo," we moaned.

"Have another drink."

"Just skip it, dude."

"She's pissed at you anyway."

"It's like fifteen minutes of dance."

"You need to go all the way back to Chicago just for that?"

"You'll just make her nervous."

"Aren't her parents gonna be there?"

"Definitely a long dinner with her parents in your future."

"I know how much you love her dad."

"Have fun with that, buddy."

"Why don't you grow a pair and stay another night?"

We threw everything at him we could think of.

"You guys are pretty funny," Ryan said, shaking the sand off the T-shirt in his hands. "Neil, let's go," he said. "You're my ride."

Neil turned to the rest of us.

"Guys, come with me."

We groaned.

"You think you're staying here while I take him to the train? Let's go, I'm the one who drove us all up here anyway."

We moaned and grumbled but dragged the cooler and chairs away from where the tide might claim them, then trudged up the staircase after Neil and Ryan.

It seems strange in hindsight, given that we knew what was about to happen, that we made the show of things that we did. Had we forgotten? Were we each pretending to ourselves that we hadn't done the thing we did? Was our play at convincing Ryan to stay some ploy at giving ourselves plausible deniability later on? Had we each, on our own, already decided that we'd never admit to him what we'd done?

When we got back upstairs, Ryan again checked the timetables on the fridge. There were two schedules: one hung beneath an oversized magnet that said SATURDAY, and beside it, one hung beneath a magnet that said SUNDAY. Neil's grandparents had laminated the schedules—a stream of children, nephews, cousins, and friends were always coming from the city to stay with them for a night or two, and the train was the quickest way. Ryan ran his thumb down the schedule.

"Train's at four," he said. "Let's get going."

We left at 3:40. The station was ten minutes away. We sat in silence on the ride over, drowsy from the sun, the windows partway down, the breeze much cooler now.

Looking out at the tall trees and the small plots of land and the teardrop trailers and shotgun houses that lined that stretch of road, I was reminded that it was November. The sun was already lower than the tops of the trees, the light had diminished, the day was darkening, and you could almost tell from the smell of the air that it was over: today would be the last of the warmth; fall would be brief; a long winter was on its way.

Ryan grabbed his duffel and scooted out as soon as we got to the station. The station clock said 3:53. We didn't pull away.

Caesar and I sat in the back. Neil caught our eyes in the rearview mirror. We smiled nervously.

Ryan was talking to the ticket seller. He was leaned way in to the seller's booth, as if trying to get a look for himself at something on the man's computer. Something was taking longer than it should.

It was 3:57. The tracks were empty in both directions as far as you could see.

Now Ryan was yelling. He had stepped back from the window and was gesturing emphatically toward the tracks. He had turned his hat around.

We opened our doors. Neil got out.

"What's up?" Neil yelled.

Ryan said something else to the ticket seller, picked up his bag, and started running over.

"Train's not fucking coming," Ryan said.

"What do you mean?" said Neil. "The schedule said 4:00 PM."

And I think, in that moment, that Neil made the decision for all of us.

"Yeah well your schedule's fucking wrong or else that guy is lying to me. And the train's not here, so I guess he's not."

The station clock said 4:03.

What we had done—and Neil's answer meant that we were never going to admit it to Ryan—was to switch the timetables on the fridge. Early that morning, when Ryan was still sleeping.

I don't remember exactly whose idea it was or who had been the one to switch them, but that is what we did: On Sundays, the trains ran every hour to accommodate the crush of people going back to the city. On Saturdays, when most people stayed put, they only ran every three hours. Today was Saturday. We'd swapped the magnets on the fridge, so the "Saturday" schedule Ryan looked at showed the trains running more often than they did. The afternoon train had come at three. The next one wouldn't leave till six.

"I can't miss this audition," Ryan said. "I can't miss her audition. I can't miss her audition," he said, and he didn't stop saying it—like a child will keep repeating how much he's been hurt—until he was crying.

Much later, when the significance of that day to the lives of each of us began to take on the fullness of its shape, when, through time and distance, its magnitude became apparent, I began thinking about the word "irrevocable," and how it seemed to fit what it was that we had done, and about how close that word is to another word, "irrecoverable."

Though we couldn't name it then, I think in hindsight that is what we sensed: that our actions that day had irrevocably summoned into the world a set of consequences, and that the guilt flooding our chests was an awareness that somewhere in the distance of our lives—of mine and Caesar's, of Neil's and Ben's, of David's and Ryan's—there now existed something that didn't exist before—something that we'd wrought—and though we couldn't say exactly what it might be, we were now moving irrevocably toward it. I have come to believe that there existed for Ryan a different life—one, I imagine, in which we never switched the timetables, and so never interfered with his relationship with Jana—a life in which, because of that, he never joined the military, a life in which they stayed together, got married, and together grew old—a life that, because of our actions, was irrecoverable now, because it would never be lived.

We hadn't known that Ryan would be so upset. I don't mean to use that as an excuse. But I say it to explain that what we had done we had done as a prank, but also, in some perverse and selfish way, because we loved him, and loved being there all together, and wanted him to stay. We didn't understand how malicious it had been until we saw his anguish.

Neil's car was the only way left to get back to the city, but it was already 4:15. We slung our arms over Ryan's shoulder, we swore up and down that Jana would forgive him, we said it wasn't his fault, we even offered to get on speakerphone with Jana to explain.

"But," we told him, "no matter how much you hope it will, driving won't get you back in time."

It would be evening by the time we approached the city, and traffic on a Saturday would be a gridlock. The audition was at seven. We'd never get there by then. The ETA said well over three hours.

Despite everything we said, Ryan put it this way to Neil: "Either you're driving me, or I'm taking your car and driving myself."

They sped off toward the interstate as the rest of us began the cold walk home to Neil's grandparents. We stayed the night, gathered the things that Neil had left behind, and hiked back to the station the next day to catch the morning train to Chicago.

Ryan and Neil hit gridlock traffic just past the toll bridge, as Neil had said they would. And by the time they pulled up to the concert hall—Ryan in the dusk, trotting up the wide stone staircase of the theater—Jana's audition was over.

I saw a movie once where an angel waits in a field of wheat to greet you when you die. The field is so vast that it contains the path of each of our lives. Not a single one runs in a straight line. From above, you see that each path is intersected by a door. Our life leads up to it and our life leads away from it, but the door marks a change in direction—like the day in Michigan—an alteration in course whose divergence becomes visible only in the distance of time.

At the end of our life, the movie explains, that door is where the angel meets us—a greeter at the door in the wheat. The angel rises with us, and helps us see which path in the vast field was our own, and which door was ours, and on which day of our life we arrived at it, and how our path changed because of it. The angel is there to console us. The angel tells us that no matter what it was that happened, it is okay.

Jana didn't forgive Ryan, though we begged her to. Behind his back, without him knowing, we approached her like an envoy, all together at first, then one on one, time and time again over the passing months. We told her the story. We explained the trick we'd played. We told her what we'd done. We swore up and down that Ryan hadn't known, that he'd done everything he could to get to her audition, that he would've been there had it not been for us.

She said she believed us. But she said it didn't matter. She refused to speak to him. It had been his choice to leave that weekend, and she didn't forgive him.

Ryan grew apart from us. I write those words but see they aren't exactly what I mean. It's nearer to the truth to say we grew apart from him. One night in late February our senior year, drunk and with a little bag of cocaine in his pocket, he swung at a cop who'd stopped us as we walked out of the park. He spent the night in jail, but instead of teaching him a lesson, that night seemed like a door he'd been waiting for: he started drinking more. We saw him less and less. I walked into his basement one Friday afternoon to find him with four guys I'd never met, all playing Halo and most of the way through a bottle of Jameson. I had a drink with them, but the way they talked kept me quiet.

Everything they said seemed to be a challenge directed at someone else.

When we were fourteen, the autumn we first started to drink, David's sister got bat mitzvahed. There was a reception table set up after the service, its tablecloth lined with Dixie cups. The ones for kids were filled with grape juice; the ones for adults were filled with wine. Ryan caught my eye, swapped the signs, and for the next ten minutes we gulped down as many of the wine-filled cups as we could.

I remember he was wearing his pure black Pink Floyd *Dark Side of the Moon* shirt beneath his dad's black blazer. I'd always thought the rainbow colors on the chest were meant to be a comet flying through space, but standing there feeling my brain get heavy and my face get hot, I looked more closely and thought of the spray of color that comes from light passing through a diamond. The word "spectral" kept blinking in my mind. We stacked one finished cup inside another till the chatter of the voices around us swarmed. Other voices became hard to distinguish and my vision seemed to swim a bit, but I felt a comfort in the warmth from the wine.

When it was time to leave, we walked cautiously out onto the temple steps. It was a bright hot day. It was one of our first times drunk. Sunlight seemed to scream off the sheen of the passing cars, and to the left, across the park, we could see the blue of Lake Michigan shimmering white in the post-noon light. Ryan was standing next to me; on the stone steps, he stood so close I could see his chest rising and falling with his breath, his figure sharp against the heat and the light.

I can remember him clearly there, whereas everything that happened our senior year comes in flashes: Ryan passing like a streak through Andrew Scaglioni's living room. Ryan huffing from a balloon filled with nitrous oxide, then flat on his back on the bedroom floor. He came to like drugs as much as he liked to drink. By the time we graduated I barely saw him anymore, though of course I heard the stories: arrested on Clark Street; whiskey on his breath in morning assembly; suspended for a week; threatened to be held back while the rest of us got ready to go to college.

Late in the spring our senior year, Ryan showed up to a party in Devon's backyard and told us he'd enlisted. Surrounded by guys we played hockey with, and girls we'd known since we'd been young, we made a spectacle: Ricky got blind drunk and sat on the stairs in tears, crying like Ryan was dead. Caesar gripped Ryan's face between his hands as Ryan tried to fight him off. Shirts were torn. Everyone who wasn't us was pushed to the sidelines. It's embarrassing to recollect.

In hindsight I see how our grand reaction only made clear how little we knew. All over the country boys our age were making the same decision as Ryan was: enlisting in the military to find community, fulfill a sense of duty, or just have something to do. Free college when they came back; American flags stamped by their names on their high school graduation pamphlets.

But in our school, where war existed mostly as a moral question, or as pictures from history, and in the stock opposition to it we inherited from our parents, Ryan was the only person anyone knew who went. He enlisted, and people assumed it was a death sentence. He enlisted, and he was judged for it.

All night we performed the scene we thought we were supposed to: Caesar tried to talk him out of it. Ricky crashed through the screen on the back door and fell asleep in the garden. The girls, recognizing our performance for what it was, went back to what they were doing. In a few months I'd go off to Pomona, Caesar to Indiana. We'd play hockey, come home every summer, keep our grades up, drink on weekends, take the internships we knew would please our parents.

Knowing now who we've each become, I look back at that night and think how out of any of us, it was Ryan who had the confidence to live his life in a way that was least beholden to what was expected of him. I respect him for that.

At summer's end, we went off to college. Ryan deferred his enlistment for a year and took a job working at Walmart and the occasional class at a community college; he got a DUI. He stayed in the job for nearly a year, and when fall came, as he'd threatened, he went to basic. He'd do two tours in Afghanistan over the next five years, the two wars creeping deeper into the new millennium, morphing into occupations, the twentieth century growing long. By the time Ryan came home, he hadn't spoken with any of us since that sweltering evening in Chicago after my freshman year of college, when we drank beers in the car in the lot behind my parents' house, and I gave him the book of war stories I'd later find crushed beneath the passenger's mat, and, before he left that night, tried to embrace him.

Remember Sam?

My girlfriend in middle school who cried like Katharine Hepburn as I held her in the bathroom at her older sister's party? Sam who said I didn't love her the same way Ryan loved Jana? She was living in New York, apparently: I recognized her immediately as I stepped out the front door of Ben's Airbnb in Cobble Hill. I was twenty-five by then, and I hadn't known she lived there.

Along with David and Caesar, I'd descended on New York for a three-day weekend. Ben's rich grandfather was getting remarried, and we were Ben's "plus three." I know that isn't the typical term, but I guess you're allowed three guests instead of one when you're related to a guy so wealthy he had a specific Rolex—as Ben told it—that he wore when he played tennis and at no other time. A watch for every occasion? Something like that.

Anyway, Ben's grandfather had gotten all that money in the stock market trading Corn Futures, though honestly I'm not sure what that is. He'd bought Ben a book for his twenty-first birthday about "ethical investing" with a note that said, DO YOUR RESEARCH! The book had a tagline that went, "You Can Do Good and Make Money Too," which made me laugh when Ben showed me, but probably isn't without some sliver of truth.

By then, Ben was in the first year of a hard job that he'd be in for the next ten, helping build affordable but genuinely nice housing in downtown districts of midsize East Coast cities; essentially luxury apartments earmarked for people in or near poverty as a means of drawing people back to vacated urban centers. It was an interesting idea and the job came with a decent salary, at least for the nonprofit world. At the wedding I'd get drunk and try to make a joke to Ben's grandfather about it being a good job, "but nothing like a Corn Future." Unsurprisingly it didn't really land, and I was left grinning by the punch bowl as Ben's granddad pretended to notice a cousin he needed to say hello to on the other side of the room.

But I was saying about Sam: I recognized her immediately as I walked out of our Airbnb and saw her coming up the street. I stepped quickly back in, hoping she hadn't seen me.

"Graham!"

Turns out she had.

Sam at twenty-four on a Friday evening in the twilight of a Brooklyn street. She looked beautiful. A sash of her dark blonde hair was dyed bright pink, and she still had the same little roundness in her shoulders when she walked, like she was tensing herself against a perpetual rain.

"What are you doing here?" she asked me, a little out of breath.

Standing before her, I felt this sudden vertigo, or disorientation; it had been so long since I'd seen her.

"Oh, you know, taking the waters," I responded, trying to make some kind of joke, though it didn't make any sense.

"Ha ha," she said. "But really. What are you doing in New York, goon? I've missed you."

Goon, I thought, nearly laughing. That was so much like her. She was always using unexpected nicknames like that, odd but endearing.

"I'm a plus three," I said.

"What?" she said again.

Another awful joke. What was wrong with me?

"It's a long story," I said. "I'm here with Ben for the weekend. Ben's grandfather's getting remarried," I explained. "David's here too."

"It's so good to *see* you," she said.

She was peering at me closely, her eyes roving back and forth across my face as she took me in. As she looked at me, I felt myself becoming hyperconscious that we were standing in the very center of the sidewalk, and that we had been for some time.

"Can we"—I said—"the people," and reached my hand toward her elbow to nudge her gently out of the path of someone walking up behind her.

We moved onto the curb, the streetlamp's cone of yellow light falling on her hair. Her eyes didn't leave my face as she adjusted the tote bag slung over her shoulder.

"You look the *same*, Graham," she said. "But older."

I was uncomfortable. Sam had that effect on me. Like Ryan when we'd been in high school, I felt Sam saw through me in a way others did not. I'd known her for so long. I'd always felt that she could see, without asking, if I was distracted or if something was wrong, even if I denied it when she asked me what it was.

"I really love the pink," I said, nodding at her hair.

She nodded back and asked, "Where are you going right now?"

I looked at my watch like I had somewhere I needed to be, but in truth Ben was at the rehearsal dinner, Caesar had gone for a run, and David had left to meet Sofia, his girlfriend at the time, and the person he would eventually marry.

We started walking.

"We could get a drink?" I offered. Dinner seemed like more time than I hoped to spend together, and at that moment I felt like I could use one.

"Sure," she said. "*You* can get a drink."

There was a tone in her voice. I looked over.

"*Graham*," she said.

"*Samantha*," I snapped back, not seeing a reason for her irritation.

"I'm sober," she said.

I kept walking, but she had stopped on the sidewalk, and it took me a second to realize she was no longer beside me. I turned to look at her.

Her head was bent and her loose hair was blowing behind her in the wind. She walked up to where I stood but looked at me like, *Where is your head? Where have you been?*

I was flustered.

"You are?" I said. "How?"

"Sorry," I added, realizing that might be taken the wrong way. "I don't mean 'how' like, 'How are you sober?,' but 'how' like, 'How would I have known that?' It's been, what, two years since we've talked?"

She looked, suddenly, very tired.

"From Ryan," she said. "I thought he'd told you. And four," she added.

"Four what?"

This wasn't going well.

"Since we've talked," she said. "The weekend in Pomona. Four years since then, not two."

The weekend in Pomona. Oh God. Not a very happy couple of nights.

I had been a senior in college. Sam had taken a gap year after high school and her path, since then, had been a little bumpy: she'd started then stopped at the same college twice and was living, at that time, with her aunt in San Francisco. I received a text from her one morning saying she was living out west, and would it be okay if she came to see me for a weekend.

Of course! I wrote. *It'll be so good to see you*, I added, but then deleted it, and what I sent instead was, *It'll be great to catch up.*

Hearing from her, I thought immediately of those hard weeks in high school that followed the night she cried against me in her bathroom, when it had been plain to both of us that there was something that existed between Ryan and Jana that would never exist between us.

It hadn't mattered that we both knew that breaking up was the right thing—a million teen movies and what we'd witnessed of our own friends' breakups had taught us a script that was expected when two people separate: fights, long silences on late-night phone calls, the significant, red-eyed glances we cast at each other as we sat in assembly. The weeks after her sister's party, we played our parts in that pageantry we'd learned, a pageantry that most of us continue to act out, in one way or another, our entire lives.

Catch up. That had seemed more neutral to me than *It'll be so good to see you*, less suggestive, and a way to nudge the way we spoke more toward the register of friendship, and less toward the intimacy of former lovers, if it's even apt to use that word: we were hardly even teenagers when we'd been together.

It'll be great to catch up, I'd sent, and messaged with a follow-up to get a better sense of what was going on, and why exactly she wanted to come. But all I came away with was a feeling that she was having a hard time. So I'd said yes, the week passed swiftly, and there Sam was, stepping off a Greyhound bus in the hot sun of Los Angeles on a Friday afternoon.

That was November 2008. Barack Obama had just been elected, and the campus was electric. The Tuesday before Sam came had been the day of the election, and it was clear by early evening on the west coast that Senator Obama was going to be our next president. It still makes me glow a little to think of it: everyone crowded around the boxy televisions in the campus common rooms; all the televisions tuned to CNN or NBC as the results poured in.

Ohio, North Carolina, Indiana, Iowa. As the night got later, the televisions showed a map of the country, the blue at the edges moving steadily inward, like the spread of an oil spill or an advancing army. By 8:00 PM on the West Coast, they'd called the election for Senator Obama. We went apeshit. Everyone did. It still gives me chills to remember.

People wept. When the election was called, people wept where they sat. People opened their dorm-room windows and howled out into the California night. They called to one another in glee as they streamed out onto the grass of the campus commons, embracing like people on the platform of a train station reuniting after years of war, and war was a real part of it: death tolls had been rising in Iraq and Afghanistan. Weapons of mass destruction hadn't been discovered, and never would be. President Bush had instigated a troop surge in 2007, and nothing had budged. Then the economy had crashed. People were tired. People were suffering.

It's hard to describe how hopeful that moment was. Fireworks rose from the lawn behind the library; we filled water bottles with tequila and our backpacks with as much beer as we could carry; and out on the vast lawn we hugged each other speechlessly, we screamed, we looked at each other and tried to speak, then just shook our heads in gratitude and relief: McCain had been defeated. Bush would soon be out of office. Barack Obama had been elected. After eight years of fear and war, we'd elected the first Black president in the country's history. We felt as though we'd survived the worst of it. We felt as though a corner had been turned. And it was into that environment that Sam arrived.

My friends from high school were surprised when I admitted to them in our group text that she was coming to stay with me.

Sam from freshman year of high school?? they asked. *We didn't even know you guys still talked.*

But in the two years Sam and I had been together, we'd grown closer than I'd ever let them know. She'd lived with her mother, mostly. Her father was an alcoholic. Her mother was sick too, almost immobile from depression. It wasn't a happy home, and Sam, when we'd been young, had come to rely on me.

The evening Sam arrived at Pomona, our hockey team had organized a bonfire in the backyard of the Hockey House to celebrate the election news, and because it was a good excuse to drink.

Sam didn't seem pleased.

"We're going to a party tonight?" she said skeptically.

We were in the car I'd borrowed to pick her up and now were on our way to the grocery store to get firewood and food. I felt nervous. It wasn't clear to me what she wanted, or why she was there.

As we browsed the grocery aisles, I asked her questions about people we'd known in high school, her sister and her mom, her life in San Francisco, how she was spending her time there. I was searching for a common ground, a thread of conversation that could help us find an ease between us after so many years, and to get a better sense of why she'd written me out of the blue.

"I mostly go and see a lot of movies," she said.

"I love that," I said, and suddenly I was reminded how much, like me, Sam loved films. It was something that we'd done together: huddled under the blankets in the corner of her mother's couch, watching movie after movie together, as young as we'd been.

We watched things that in hindsight seem solidly mainstream, but at the time seemed indie, or edgy, like we were older than our years: *Wonder Boys, Almost Famous*, this foreign one we stumbled on and came to love called *My Life as a Dog*.

It's about a boy in Scandinavia who loses his parents, or, for reasons I can't remember, comes to live without them. I can hardly remember a thing about it now, except that the boy's refuge is a tree house, in a clearing in the woods. He hides up there when things are hard; he lights a candle; he thinks about that space dog, Laika, who was sent off into the cosmos and never came back.

I get sad when I think about that dog: an agent-less little creature being launched into space without his agreement or consent, his breath slowly leaving his body as he grows older, year by year, and year by year his spaceship travels farther and farther from our small blue home.

Sam said she loved it—going to see movies each afternoon—but as we walked out of the grocery store, the pastel sunset spreading wide over the parking lot, I wasn't left with a good feeling.

I wouldn't have been able to put it like this back then—I didn't have the words for it, or couldn't see Sam clearly enough to understand—but I now have the sense that Sam had come to see me that weekend because she wanted to be looked at more closely. I believe that she sensed that something was very wrong in her life, and hoped that I might ask her about it. I think she hoped that in spending time with me—who'd once been so familiar with her life—I might ask something that would get to the center of what was going on with her, and she could finally unburden herself.

At that time, however, all I was able to put my finger on was that Sam was unhappy. She was scared, she told me. The gap year had mostly been a delay to put off the anxiety of applying for college. Her senior year of high school, she said, her anxiety had been so crippling that on the day she had to take the SAT, she'd run to the bathroom and thrown up halfway through, then returned to the testing room and gotten her things and left.

That happened twice. Finally, she decided she'd just get her diploma and put the test off for a while by taking the gap year. She completed the test eventually, but her experience with it, and seeing her friends go off to school while she herself stayed back, unmoored her a little bit, or evaporated her confidence: when she finally applied to and started college, something wouldn't stick. She started, stopped, tried again, dropped out. She'd spent the most recent summer with a volunteer program in Ethiopia. At its end she had come back to the States, moved in with her aunt in San Francisco, and was now trying to manage a long-distance relationship with a boy she'd met in the program. The boy she was seeing was rich, and lived in New York City. From what she said, he wasn't very kind to her. He kept saying he'd come to see her in California, but he still hadn't. I felt sorry.

On the ride to the party, she asked if we could stop at a liquor store. I laughed.

"There's going to be plenty of booze there," I assured her.

But she said she still liked to drink Mike's Hard Lemonade, and knew there wouldn't be any at the party.

"Can we just stop and get some?" she snapped. "Is that an inconvenience?"

Mike's Hard. That had been her favorite when we were young: when we went to parties, that was all she drank.

It would have been endearing to me that she still liked it best, but I watched her finish two in the front seat before we even got to the party, and she was opening a third by the time we walked in the door.

That was, unfortunately, the Sam that I'd known. Maybe it should've set off an alarm, but at the time, the way she drank didn't really surprise or worry me. Since she'd been in eighth grade, that had been our pattern. We'd all started drinking so early and so heavily it would be a long time before anyone was able to distinguish what was normal and what was not.

When we were teenagers, and even that weekend in Pomona. I had no reason to think that there was anything abnormal about the way I drank, or the way that Sam did, though when we were younger there'd been hints. Small disasters had seemed to befall us. I once watched her face register her finger break as she leaned against the bathroom door at Heather Marie's graduation party—a wide astonished gasp I will never forget spread across Sam's face as her finger was closed in the jamb. There'd been a sprained ankle too, or a broken one, though all I can remember is that it happened on a beach, and that we tried and failed to sneak our drinks with us into the hospital waiting room. And for me, a hundred small injuries, little scrapes on my forehead, or just anxiety overriding my sleep when I'd wake on a Saturday after drinking all night Friday, only three hours remaining until I'd have to depart for my hockey game.

As we walked into the party together at Pomona that night I felt, all of a sudden, something I hadn't felt since we'd been together: responsible for someone else; trying—and I wasn't proud of it—to control their behavior; worried how drunk she might become; uneasy at what people might think of me because of her, or how she acted, as if I might be judged based on how people perceived her. I hated that in myself. It laid bare for me how thin-skinned I was.

That was not a good night, though it started well. My friends had lit a bonfire in the backyard, people were still joyful because of the election, and they'd set up a microphone and a little electric piano, the makeshift throne from which my best friend, Casey, led everyone at the party through a Power Hour sing-along.

That was something we did back then—Power Hours—and they worked like this: everyone was given a shot glass and a stash of beer; Casey would sit at the piano with a stopwatch and begin to play a song; every sixty seconds, a horn would sound and he'd begin to play a new one; each time he switched songs, everyone was meant to take a shot of the beer they were drinking. This would last for an hour—hence the name Power Hour—so at the hour's end, if you were taking the game seriously, you'd have taken sixty shots of beer.

I loved that game. It was fun to be among people committed to getting drunk, and it got us drunk. Sam with her bag of Mike's Hard played along with us, and after an hour, like all of us, she was blasted. In the glow from the fire, amid the tide of voices of college kids, themselves drunk and exuberant in the late-evening California glow, I looked over to see Sam tipping sideways in the lawn chair we'd bought at the grocery store, trying to stand up.

"Graham," she said, trying to leverage herself on the chair's thin metal arm. "I want to sing."

Good Lord.

I reached out to help her, but she had already stumbled up, knocking over her chair as she did so. A leaf was stuck to the butt of her jeans, and she walked wobbly and unsteadily toward the microphone.

And then she was standing in front of it, her magnified voice carrying out across the lawn, silencing the din of conversation. Everyone turned to look at her.

Sam is small. It's a fact about her I always forget, then am reminded of when she hugs me, the top of her head only reaching my chin, the bones of her little shoulders, her shoulders no wider than those of a slim wooden chair. Standing there in the California dusk, in the smell of flowers, beneath a high clear November sky, Sam began to sing. Standing there in the deepening evening, in the diminishing light, Sam began an a cappella rendition of that famous song by Pink Floyd, heavy and slow, with the terribly sad chorus.

It still makes my heart ache to remember that moment: the sadness and yearning with which Sam sang; that she was drunk among a bunch of strangers; that as she sang, earnest but a little off-key, it sounded as though she were pleading, or asking for forgiveness, though it was me who was sliding deeper into my lawn chair, my face hot with shame and embarrassment.

Sam sang, the river of pain in her voice so apparent that people listened. They lowered their heads. Some of my friends looked over at me. And rather than stand and clap, or cheer her on, or encourage others to do so too, and bring everyone along with me, I stayed where I sat.

Four years since that night, and here Sam was again, standing in front of me.

"I'm proud of you," I said. "For your sobriety. I really mean that. It's the first thing I should've said when you told me."

Sam put her hand on my arm. "Thank you, G. I feel lucky. I know people say it a lot, but it saved my life."

We were still standing under that streetlamp. People passed by, coming home from work, or on their way to drinks, dinner. I wanted to hear more. I wanted to know how she'd gotten sober. I wanted to understand how it was that Ryan knew she was sober when I had not.

"Do you want to walk?" I offered. "I want to hear the story."

"Sure," she said, so we turned in the direction of the Brooklyn Bridge, and she began to tell me.

The story started when she left Pomona after visiting me, though the root causes were from long before. It was a hard story to hear.

At the end of the weekend of the bonfire party she returned to San Francisco. The boy she was seeing—Misha—continued to refuse to come see her, so she followed him to New York instead. That autumn and into winter, she lived with him in the apartment his parents paid for. She applied to school in New York, got accepted, and enrolled for the spring semester.

"I have a problem with drinking," Sam said. "That was half of the start of what happened. The other half was my relationship with Misha, though obviously problems with one fed the problems with the other."

She made a sound, remembering something, and shook her head.

"It scares me whenever I look back on that time: when things were bad with him I just became another person, or I became no one at all, I don't know. I would black out and wake up in the beds of total strangers."

We were standing on Boerum Place where it turns into Brooklyn Bridge Boulevard, bright bulbs outlining the bridge's arc in the night, the broad beams in the distance rising over the water.

"Oof," she stopped. "I'm sorry. I don't know if you want to hear this, but I'm just remembering something else. This has happened a lot the longer I've been sober," she said. "Things I'd forgotten start coming back."

"What happened?" I said.

"God, Graham. I'm remembering that I woke up one time in the bed of a guy who played on the baseball team. I had literally no idea where I was. I didn't know who he was. Someone had to tell me later. I had no idea where my clothes were. They weren't in that room. The sheets around me were totally soaked. I guess I'd peed in the bed in the middle of the night."

We continued walking, crossing over to the middle of the street to access the pedestrian path that fed people up the ramp and onto the bridge.

"Things like that kept happening. Misha is such a fucking prick, and I was a mess. I did so much dumb shit. I fucked, like, a lot of people. By the time of my birthday, late July, I'd gotten pregnant. Misha wouldn't even answer my calls. He literally turned off his phone. My best friend was this girl Angie, and I had to ask her to come with me. To get an abortion, obviously. Honestly, Graham, that morning was one of the worst of my life. I couldn't stop shaking. The walls were this awful bright yellow. Weirdly I remember how much that upset me. It wasn't even the color that upset me, but that the wall was just this cheap cinder block that the clinic had painted over. It felt like a preschool. Anyway, obviously, it happens to a lot of people, or a lot of people make the same choice I made. That's not what hurt—or, at least, that's not what hurt me. It's that I didn't have any support."

Manhattan at night. The dark steel of a new building beginning to rise where the two towers once stood. It was 2012 then, and only the bottom half of the steel frame had been covered with glass. It was strange to witness: light from the city gleaming off the glass panes extending halfway up, but above that, just the pipe and steel innards of the structure, like some strange giant figure missing its skin.

Sam Sam Sam Sam Sam.

There was so much pain in her voice as she spoke. I felt sick for her. I wanted to stop where we stood, to put my arms around her and hold her close to me. I tried to speak, but could only swallow.

She looked over at me. I was glad for the darkness. My eyes were wet, and I hoped she wouldn't see.

I was remembering something else that happened the weekend she'd come to visit me. After she'd sung that song, after I'd sunk down in my chair instead of rising to support her, we'd continued to drink. We were standing in the backyard, in a circle of my friends. What exactly happened I can't remember. One of them, Casey probably, was making fun of me for something I'd done the weekend before, some hapless act or thing I'd said, and Sam joined in. She tacked something on to what he'd said, ganging up on me in a way that in that moment—less than sober, surrounded by friends I was still trying to impress, to be liked by—I didn't take kindly to, and I made a joke in return at Sam's expense.

What was it that I said? Perhaps some slight about how much she'd had to drink, or the way that, earlier, she'd sung that song, repeating the lyrics back to her in a mocking tone.

Whatever it was, I instantly regretted it. I watched her face crumple into a hurt so plain and painful it sent me immediately back to the memory of watching her cry that night in her bathroom, when we'd been teenagers.

In the aftermath of that joke, all my stupid reasons for it fell away. I saw the situation more clearly for what it was: she was surrounded by strangers in a city that was strange to her at a very difficult time in her life. They had been making fun of me, and she joined them. She was simply trying to fit in. It makes me feverishly sad to write this, to read that sentence back to myself and see the truth of how I'd behaved.

Standing with Sam on the bridge, Manhattan shining on the river's other side, I was thinking about the timeline of her story. The events with Misha that she was describing had started for her in the winter of 2009. I realized that I had been in Prague then, fairly briefly, December through February, for an abbreviated Winter Session Pomona offered for seniors interested in pursuing master's programs in public policy or international relations.

What a strange time that was to be abroad. A new American president; the middle of winter in central Europe. It probably won't surprise you to hear that I spent a lot of time there drinking. I was frozen by the beauty of the city. I got lost in it, when I had the time, walking without direction or destination, sometimes for entire days. There was a basement-level coffee shop near my dorm, where I would read or do homework. It had wood floors. You could smoke cigarettes inside. Old men came to play chess. I'd work all afternoon, drinking cappuccino, watching the slow, steady snow falling outside the windows, then I'd switch over to beer as evening came on.

But I remember vividly I had the sense of how much, back home, people were suffering. I had *The New York Times* as the home page on my browser, and sometimes at night, when I couldn't sleep, I'd sit at my desk by the high twin windows in my small dormitory bedroom, hitting *refresh, refresh* on the browser button, following the news from home.

I read this article about a city in Florida decimated by the housing bubble. The people there, the article said, had been middle class. Then the market crashed. Now, each morning, huge lines of those same people stretched endlessly down the streets, under the hot sun. They were lining up for the free bread handed out each morning at the Lutheran church. The piece described laid-off construction workers scavenging through trash bags outside a foreclosed home, searching for CDs, wire, unplugged phones—anything that could be sold. That level of desperation startled me. It seemed like it came from a bygone time. Sitting close to my computer, my face washed in the glow of the screen, those scenes felt almost unreal.

From this distance, I am able to see what a mark that was of privilege. I had the sense of how much people were suffering. But there in Prague, drinking in the Cave Bar nearly every night, smoking with classmates, ordering yet another tall dark pint, I was removed from it. I observed it from a distance. Like the events of September 11, the events I was reading about hadn't touched me—not really, anyway, not in any serious way. And not till walking through Brooklyn with Sam that night, standing beside her, crossing the East River, listening to her story, did I begin to have an understanding of the way that the beginning of her own suffering had correlated so closely with my three months in Prague, the easy life I was living there, how simultaneous those two timelines were. The contrast made my heart ache. It made me ashamed of myself.

At the bridge's middle, Sam and I stopped, crouching low to examine the locks that had been left there by lovers, hundreds and hundreds of them fastened to the railings, strung there alongside ribbons, string, colored shoelaces.

"Things got worse," Sam said. "I just stopped going to class. I couldn't handle it. My parents stopped paying tuition. Then the school wouldn't let me stay in the dorms anymore."

"Jesus," I said.

"I moved in with Angie for a little while, in Chelsea. She had an apartment with another girl. The university owned the building, so the two of them got a discount since they were still students. For like eight, ten months, I don't really know, I was just sleeping on their couch. I was just drinking. I literally didn't do anything. I was just drinking, every single night. Other things happened—I'd babysit once in a while, and made some money working part-time in a coffee shop—but that's the gist of it, that's what my life looked like.

"So what happened was," Sam continued, "my parents stopped speaking to me. Then one night near Thanksgiving—I guess it was Thanksgiving break, because Angie and the other girl had gone home to their parents—I came back to the apartment. It was really late, like 3:00 or 4:00 AM, I don't know. I was drunk.

I was more than drunk. I was blackout. I guess I was hungry, because I lit the stove, and then I don't remember anything at all. The next time I was conscious I was in the hospital. I had all these tubes in my arms, and one down my throat from them pumping my stomach. The nurses kept coming by to check on me, but no one would tell me what happened, or nobody knew. Finally one of their psych guys came by."

Sam was crying. She wiped her eyes.

"Graham," she said. "The entire kitchen burned down that night. I was so drunk the smoke didn't even wake me up. The firefighters got there in time and carried me out. They stopped the fire from spreading. I have literally zero memory of anything. I didn't wake up until the next day."

Now I put my arms around her. She let me hug her for a second, her body kind of limp in my arms, and then she stepped back.

"Is that what got you to stop drinking?" I asked.

"Not exactly," she said. "I was a mess, obviously. I left the hospital that day and went to a bar, not realizing what day it was. There was hardly anyone there, which I thought was weird. Then when the bartender came over, she said, 'Happy Thanksgiving.' I don't know what it was about that, but I just lost it. I burst into tears. I think right then and there I decided I was going to die, that I was going to end my life."

"I wrote a post on Facebook. I honestly don't think I cared if I died. I don't know what I was thinking, but I put a status update there that laid out everything. I said what had happened. I said what a mess I was; I said I'd just gotten out of the hospital; I said I was at a bar by myself on fucking Thanksgiving with zero family and zero money and zero food, that I literally had nowhere to go and no one to help me. I honestly can't believe I did that. I feel so embarrassed by it now. But it saved my life."

"How?" I said.

"Ryan," Sam said.

"Ryan what?" I asked.

"Ryan responded. He was the only one, actually, except for people responding with heart and hug emojis or whatever. I guess a few others said they were thinking of me. But he actually messaged me when he saw it. He was home on leave. He said he knew what I was going through. I honestly laughed when I read that. I didn't believe him. It sounded so cliché. But he sent a second message with his cell phone number and told me to call him. I think it was either that or I was going to die, so I did. I called him."

We followed the pedestrian path down the slope of the bridge, Manhattan looming before us like a lit-up ship.

"And Ryan did know," Sam said. What she had been going through, she meant—he really did know.

That made sense to me. The same or something similar had happened to him. I remember hearing it from Caesar—how Ryan had gotten sober while he'd been in Afghanistan. He would've been off alcohol for eight or nine months by the time he saw Sam's message that Thanksgiving afternoon in 2010.

I think a lot about that day in her life: Thanksgiving afternoon, Sam at the bar, totally alone in that huge cold city, her clothes full of smoke, sending out—like a flare from a lifeboat lost at sea—that final cry for help.

I think, sometimes, though I try my hardest not to, about what might have happened had Ryan not responded, about what she might have done. I picture her sitting there; I picture the drink she ordered sitting in front of her; I picture two paths through time extending outward from her chest: one goes toward life, one toward death.

Sam turned to me. We had descended into Manhattan, then dipped underground to catch the train back to Brooklyn. We were standing at the Wall Street stop. The platform surrounding us was empty. Sam looked around to make sure, then lit a cigarette, waving away the smoke as it drifted toward me.

"I started when I stopped drinking," she apologized. "Kills you slower than drinking will."

I laughed, then asked if I could have one.

She looked at me in surprise, then gave me the one she was smoking, and lit another. We leaned back together against the platform wall, smoking as we waited for the train.

"Ryan helped me get connected to AA," she said. "He found me a meeting to go to, that same Thanksgiving afternoon. In a library basement right around the corner from the bar, actually. I went once, then I kept going. He was my sponsor for a while, at the start. Until I found a little stability. Then he said it would be better for me if I found someone local."

"I don't know if you and your friends ever knew this," Sam continued, "but I got to know Ryan a little bit toward the end of high school. In your senior year."

I'd had no idea.

"I'd started sleeping with a friend of my sister's," Sam said. "They'd been at college together, my sister and this friend. I met him when he stopped by my mom's apartment one night to see my sister. He was done with college by then, and living in Chicago. I kept it a secret from my sister, but he and I started dating. He worked in finance. He'd take me out to nice places. One bar he liked was at the top of the Alibi Hotel. Ryan used to go there, winter and spring your senior year. Did you ever know that?"

I counted back in my head: that would've been the winter after we switched the timetables, and the silence between him and Jana it led to.

Sam continued: "Anyway, Nico and I would have dinner there. If it was a Friday or Saturday night, I usually saw him. Ryan, I mean. Drinking at the bar. I guess he must've had a fake

ID. He was drunk, usually. Very. But he'd always come over to say hello. Nico liked him."

"Nico's the guy you were dating?"

Sam nodded.

"But yeah, as drunk as Ryan would get, he always said hello to us. I don't think I ever saw him talk to anyone else. He'd just drink and look at his phone, or look at the bar, or off into space at nothing in particular. It made me sad. I was curious about him. I was curious why he was always there alone. I was curious why you guys were never with him. I was curious what happened.

"After I got sober," Sam continued, "when he and I were speaking daily for AA check-ins, I finally asked him about those nights at the hotel. He told me about the trip to Michigan, you know. The missed train and all that. And then what happened between him and Jana. I didn't know any of that back then. But I remember how sad it made me to see him sitting there each weekend, drinking by himself. Because at first I thought he must be waiting for Jana, but Jana kept not coming. Then later, after I learned what happened, I realized that he hadn't been *waiting* for Jana, because by then he would have known she wasn't coming; he'd been thinking of her."

Visit to Riverhead

The month before David and Sofia had their second kid, we all convened in Riverhead, at the crest of Long Island's split at Flanders Bay. David and Sofia had bought an old farmhouse there the summer before and turned it into their vacation home. The weekend was supposed to be a last hurrah of sorts before the arrival of their new child (I pictured a line of shots and a fridge full of Rolling Rock awaiting us when we arrived) but when I got there I found Ben alone at the kitchen sink, lost in thought, rinsing dishes as he waited for water to boil for a pot of tea.

I propped the door open with a foot and hurled my duffel bag into the foyer, then reached behind me to grab the case of beer I'd picked up on my way, but Ben, even before greeting me, came hurrying over to shush me, his finger over his lips.

"She's sleeping!" he hissed, pointing to the ceiling.

"Who's sleeping?" I responded without lowering my voice, though I knew full well he'd meant David's two-year-old daughter. The three-hour drive from Philadelphia had taken me five hours between the Pennsylvania traffic and the torrential rain through New Jersey and New York, and I was in less than a good mood about the long trip and the less-than-ceremonious welcome.

Long Island in early November in the fall of 2018: Ben in the kitchen doing dishes; David and Sofia at the train station, waiting for their daughter's nanny to arrive; Neil on his way from

Chicago, where his wife was three months pregnant; Caesar making his way by train from Boston.

I was thirty-one years old. I had fled Los Angeles to Chicago, for a time, before moving to Philadelphia, where I'd found a desk job at a nonprofit. I'd taken it as a summer job to hold me over until I found something more in line with my public policy background, but the work was easy and I felt good about it—we provided free dress clothes and interview prep to low-income job seekers—and I'd stayed on in the position when the summer ended.

Ben disappeared with my bag into some other segment of the house, and I walked through the quiet rooms, touching the handsome weathered tabletops, admiring the wide wood boards of the floor.

I'd stayed there before, but each time I came back I'd walk those rooms, astonished all over again: it remains, I think, the most beautiful home I've ever slept in. It had been built forever ago, so the ceilings were low and the walls stone and thick, and each room was wide and warm. The big open den had the feeling of a cavern, or a tavern, and I sank down in the cushions of a well-worn armchair that was pushed up close to the gaping brick face of the fireplace.

I sat there with my eyes closed for a few moments, trying to slow my breathing and will my beating heart to come to rest. I loved that house, but I was always anxious in the days leading up to going there. David and Sofia, one daughter and a son on the way, a house in New Haven and another on Long Island: their lives seemed so grand and adult, so polished and intentional in comparison to mine. I had failed to finish my grad program; my life in Los Angeles had been a mess, and so I'd fled; I'd found some stability in Philadelphia, but it seemed like every time I arrived at their house in New Haven, or came to see them on Long Island, I was never the version of myself I hoped to be. I was always hungover, or had a cold, or hadn't slept well, or had squeezed in time to see them on a Sunday morning after a weekend spent at bars with friends. I wanted them to see me as funny, kind, reliable, yet every time I came over I was already split in my mind, one part trying to mitigate the effects of too little sleep or too much drinking, a big part struggling to be the person I wanted them to see me as, the third part observing myself trying and failing to be the person the second part wanted me to be.

They both came from big families and their houses were often full of children—young sons and daughters of their siblings or their cousins—and I'd find myself stumbling over my words, constantly faltering on the children's names, saying Mike when I meant to say Sal or Gus when I meant to say Vic, though on that last count I kind of forgave myself: my friends were all anointing their children with names that would have fit a Philadelphia mob family in the 1930s, and I couldn't keep the kids straight. There were two named "Sal" and one named "Lou" and both a "Joe" and a "Joe Jr.," and two-year old Vic, very confusingly, had a cousin named Vickie. The first time I met David and Sofia's daughter I'd hungoverly called her the name of David's sister's child. That had not gone over well.

This time, I was proud of myself. In the days leading up to this visit I'd slept well, I'd limited my drinking, and the night before I got there I hadn't even had a single beer. But then the drive up to Long Island was madness: heavy traffic as I left Philadelphia; heavy rain crossing through New York; a series of road closures past Westbury that left me turning in a circle, trying to find a different route north, finally arriving after five hours of driving only to find Ben making a pot of tea, meeting me with such a stern and brief greeting that I felt stung.

Where was everyone? Just as I wondered, the back door opened—cold air, shuffling feet, laughter—and then the whole house seemed to suddenly brighten with sound. I playfully peeked my head around the armchair as they all entered, like a hiding child, and truly everyone was there: not just David and Sofia and their nanny, Sylvia, but Caesar and Neil too, and I walked into the foyer to greet them.

"Kaaaaatz," Caesar said. He was wearing a black peacoat and pulling a green beanie off his head, his face ruddy from the cold air.

"Come here, babe, how are you?" he said, and gave me a hug, and then Neil did, and then David and Sofia, and then someone made a joke about why were we crowded in the foyer when there was such a big house around us, so we followed each other out into the den, and then the kitchen, asking questions about travel, flights and trains, the rooms lit warm and brightly, soft and yellow against the invisible night.

It was easy to fall back into the rhythm of being with each other. Thirteen years since high school, but in the interim we'd kept reasonably close, descending on Chicago for school breaks and vacations around the holidays, convening at the corner bar, drinking freezing pints of Old Style from thick glass mugs in the comfort of the dim tavern.

I was sore at Ben for the cold welcome, and sore at David too, though he didn't know it. A month earlier he'd forwarded an email to all our friends that had itself been forwarded to him. The original email had been written by Sam. It had somehow made its way to David, but she had originally meant it for just a small group of her friends and cousins in New York, explaining that she was paying her way through nursing school, and could really use some money, and was looking for a part-time job. She talked about her experience being a nanny, and asked the people on the email to get in touch if they needed someone to look after their kids, or if they knew anyone who did. David's forward arrived in my inbox without any accompanying text, just a face emoji with a raised eyebrow, as if he was saying, "Look where she ended up."

I was so angry when I received that email. David had forwarded it to all of us: not only to me, but to Caesar, Ben, and Neil too, though he knew full well none of us lived in New York and so couldn't be of help to Sam in the way she needed. I felt he'd sent it just to poke fun at her, or to get our friends to share memories of when Sam and I had dated forever ago, knowing the guys loved to rag me about that. Whatever his reasons were, forwarding that email seemed so mean-spirited to me. I had gotten halfway through an email back to him, then decided against it, but here is what I'd written:

> *I wish you hadn't sent that. It seemed mean-spirited and I don't see much of a plausible reason why you'd send it to all of us if not to make fun of her, though what you're making fun of I'm not really sure, since it seems an earnest attempt by someone who needs money to find some work that can help her get through school.*

Even reading that back to myself, I feel this great anger rising in my chest. David—and the same was true for the rest of us—would never have to worry about money in the way that Sam did for a single day in his entire life. I pictured him in handsome slacks, his slim black cell phone in his hand, sending that message off to us and then, with a brush of his thumb, swiping Sam's life off his screen forever with the same light touch he'd use to open up another window in the browser, the new page blooming with the day's news, new restaurants to go to, the line graphs of the market indexes showing promise. The incongruous scales of her need and his flippancy—as I imagined it—enraged me. If not to mock her circumstance, why had he forwarded us her message?

In the end I hit *save* on my email draft rather than *send*, and closed my computer.

First night on Long Island, everyone together again after nearly a year apart. Sofia, as busy as she was caring for their kid, had ordered Indian food for all of us, and after I'd showered in the little upstairs bathroom—its window looked out onto distant woods, a closer field, and nearer, the low wall of handsome stone that enclosed the home's backyard—I walked down to the first-floor den to find the food arrayed on a plum-and-yellow afghan Sofia had laid across the length of an old leather trunk. There were candles and open bottles of wine spaced among the dishes, and we sat on the floor's thick warm rug in the low glow of the heavy candles, dipping naan into the bowls of steaming curries and sauces.

It was wonderful. Wonderful to sit there on the floor; wonderful, in the buzz of the liquor, to take in the deep greens and umbers of the food, the apple red and burnt orange of the bowls in which it was served; wonderful to be among friends, so at ease with one another; wonderful to lean back for a moment out of the shimmer of the candlelight, to sip wine in silence and to feel the peace of the house around us, the peace of being around this table, beside these people who I loved, our shoes piled by the door like shoes kicked off by children grateful to be home.

It was less wonderful to discover that in my revery I'd had five glasses of wine, made evident when I made a lurching reach for the open bottle and almost toppled the chana masala. But why not? We hadn't been together in months. David and Sofia's second baby was on the way. We were celebrating.

"Who needs another?" I asked, interrupting Caesar as he explained the difference between a "dividend" and a "distribution" and some apparent relation those terms had to the bankruptcy of a business he was consulting for in Mexico City. Everyone made a polite check of their mostly full glasses and turned back to Caesar.

"They're fucking idiots," he continued, "but it won't impact me. We gave them a blueprint and they didn't follow it, so we still get paid, and I'll just be moved to a different project."

He was wearing an emerald-green sweater with the collar of a maroon oxford visible above the neckline, elegantly disheveled, like someone handsome having a drink at a bar after leaving the office. He seemed so well put together. Each of them did: Neil in simple baggy barrel pants that cinched tight around the ankle, a vintage Polo hoodie on top; Ben in his usual outfit, dressed like you'd dress for Christmas dinner with a girlfriend's father; David at ease in his home, in his Jetsetter tech pants and ocher Sabahs, rolling a joint to enjoy after dinner. I thought, for a moment, of those champagne nights in high school at Tish's mother's apartment—Tish straddling Caesar on the couch, Sidney dropping gummi bears into Ryan's waiting mouth, David so drunk he was rolled up in the rug, babbling something at Neil. How far they all had come.

The person who was missing, of course, was Ryan. I couldn't help but think of his absence, even if we didn't speak about it. But I also thought, *Why would we speak of it?* We were just beginning sophomore year of college when he left for basic, then no one saw him again until after graduation. While he was in basic in San Diego, we were home from college for fall break. When he left San Diego for specialized training, we were in Chicago, doing Jäeger bombs in Caesar's mother's basement. First in college and then in the years after, even with the distance between the places we came to live, we remained close, holidays in Chicago bringing us back together, pacing the years like the skips of a stone across the face of a river.

It was different with Ryan. He was first in Munich, then Afghanistan—in Bamyan or Baghlan—provinces whose names we tried to pronounce with casual confidence, like we knew anything about them. He couldn't really call, and we didn't call him. His parents moved to Denver his first year in the marines, so when he did come home on leave it was no longer Chicago that he came home to. His life, the longer that passed since I'd seen him in person, became vague and narrow to me: without updates and detail, my sense of him became drained of color, till he'd become just the Ryan of my memories and that picture of him in his marine uniform I'd once seen on Facebook. I mean to say that, for my friends, what happened with Ryan—the trick we played in Michigan and the dissipation of our friendship—had grown small in their memory, as it had, for a time, in my own, until that night in Brooklyn when I ran into Sam. That was what had got me thinking of him again.

We brought the dishes to the kitchen, dumped what remained of the food, then Sofia shooed us out to the screened-in porch, claiming she needed us out of her hair. Sofia was a force: one child sleeping upstairs and another on the way, and neither pregnancy nor motherhood had slowed her down a bit. She worked in media and had made an almost mythic reputation for herself crafting ad campaigns that were known for their bizarre, dreamlike logic, and their unlikely effectiveness: their individual elements confounded people—no one could precisely define why they worked—but viewers were riveted by them, and more often than not, came away wanting to buy the thing being sold. And in life, the person behind them was open, warm, and full of grace: her admonishment to leave the kitchen was of course her way of saying, "Go drink, go talk, go be together, you have my blessing."

David grabbed his bag of weed, Caesar, Ben, and Neil took a beer each from the fridge, and I brought out to the porch the bottle of whiskey I'd brought with me from Philly.

How many nights had we spent like that? A back porch, starlight, a table, enough beer to erase any fear that the beer could run out.

Sitting there, suddenly, the flood of all that time together swept over me like a wave. I was overtaken: suitcases of mental Polaroids spilling open, the feeling of summer evenings easing slowly into night; Jana on the shore of the lake, turning back toward Ryan, the fury of her hair flashing red against the blue. I thought of Michigan, the screened-in porch at Neil's grandparents', all of us growing brown beneath the summer sun. All together back then in an unspecific August, our conversation being blown away into the hum of the insects in the gathering dusk, the endless wash of the lake reaching up to us from somewhere down the bluff.

And then I was back where I was: the suburbs of Long Island, not in need of whiskey but pouring whiskey anyway, then offering it to my friends, though David, then Ben, then Neil, then Caesar each declined.

"Gotta stay clearheaded for the hike in the morning," said Ben.

I had not been informed about a hike.

"Very funny," I said.

"I wasn't joking," said Ben. "We took one before you got here today. It'll be good for you," he said, giving a little nod toward my drink.

I wasn't sure what he meant by that and in that moment did not want to ponder it too deeply.

"Yeah, well, the night is young," I said. "We'll see how ready for a hike you are tomorrow after you've had a few more beers."

Ben gave a look I'd seen from him before, something between mocking and skeptical, that was more for the other guys than it was for me, and it meant, "That's not likely."

David jumped in. He reached a hand out and patted Neil's knee and said, "So tell us about the new promotion. Seems promising for that down payment, huh?"

The context was that Neil's wife was three months pregnant, and they'd begun looking for a house to buy in their neighborhood in Chicago.

I felt myself recede a little bit. I felt my mind churning with a wash of complicated thoughts. I felt a little out of place. I felt, I think, genuine gladness for what was happening in the lives of my friends, but I felt sad too: their lives looked so different from my own. Their lives had shifted so much, it seemed to me, and astonishingly quickly: it had hardly been two years since Neil and I had been booted by the bouncer from a bar in Chicago on New Year's Eve, ditched our coats in the alley around the corner, swapped hats, took off our glasses, and tried to get back in wearing just our T-shirts, convinced the bouncer wouldn't recognize us. Now Neil was in a weekly class where he was quizzed on the "Baby Basics of Safe Sleep" and texting us literature from the class curriculum explaining the merits of something called "Tummy Time."

I know, I know, I sound like someone bitter at being left behind, and perhaps that was a part of it, but top to bottom my heart was full of gladness that these people who I loved were creating for themselves the lives they said they wanted. Even if I felt some whiplash at how quick the change had happened, I felt happiness: though it didn't look exactly like a fun life to me—having children; the way that seemed to insert a new center at the lives of my friends who had them—it seemed a noble one.

Unlike me, they'd made choices. They'd been able to see with clarity a few specific things they wanted—kids, a home, growing old among family—with a surety that I admired, and that I hadn't found in my own life. David and Sofia, Neil and Neil's wife: their lives were organized (or would be soon in Neil's case) around something beyond them. In centering their children, they didn't live solely for their own whims and desires, as I felt I was doing at that time, and I admired them for that.

Still, I didn't think I wanted that for myself. I don't mean to say I felt I'd found some secret to living or anything—I was a disaster, in some ways. It had only been a few months prior that Ben had driven down to Philly to watch the Kentucky Derby with me. I was in a string, at that time, of weeks whose weekends I didn't seem able to escape without drinking leading to me doing something I regretted, and the weekend of Ben's visit proved to be no different. I remember standing with him in the kitchen at the end of the night, swaying as I tried to explain the disgust I felt at the way I drank. I didn't even feel drunk by then, I just felt in despair of myself. Which is to say I was a mess, as Sam had once called me, Nina too, though she had said it fondly.

In comparison to my friends, my life seemed uncentered, fuzzy, erratic. I felt I was living solely for myself. To reach outside myself, I read the Bible. I tried to pray. I'd turn off my phone and read novels for hours on end, or listen to Mahler.

I saw this movie once that takes place in summer. The visiting grad student sleeps with his professor's teenage son. I loved the world of that film, and the way the teenage kid would spend his time: transcribing music, taking a bike ride, swimming in a freezing lake, lying on his attic mattress in the sweltering afternoons and touching himself. I'd do this thing where I tried to think of myself as him. As I smoked a cigarette, as I lay with my eyes closed and listened to a symphony, I imagined myself as the kid in the movie, my life as his life, elegant in summer green. It's strange to say, but it helped me. I felt more present. I felt as if I wasn't alone. I felt as if something beyond me was watching.

I tried, as part of that feeling, to volunteer, delivering boxes of food to people in need, senior citizens in Philadelphia living on their own. I caught a glimpse of purpose in that work, the glow that comes from doing something for others even when you don't really want to. I would've rather been doing something else, but I came to cherish those afternoons driving through the city, hauling the heavy boxes to the doorsteps of different houses, trotting back to my idling car, the little wave of thanks I'd sometimes get as people retrieved them, leaning out from their half-open doors.

But most weekends I failed to follow through, waking on Sunday with a headache the size of the moon, burying my head beneath my pillows, going back to sleep. Without anything outside myself truly obligating me, it made it easy to turn away.

I was in a bad pattern, but still I saw that I wouldn't have swapped my friends' lives for my own. I recalled having dinner with my parents the summer before. Neil's father had joined us—my parents had known him as long as I'd known Neil—and I remember feeling criticized, though inadvertently, as he spoke about some of the people I'd grown up with, giving updates on where they were, what they were doing, who they had married. I was single. I had been for five years, and I remember his exact phrasing:

"They all seem good," he'd said. "They're good, well-adjusted kids. They're doing what they're supposed to be doing: getting married, having children, building a future."

I think that was what nagged at me. He'd spoken out loud the quiet expectation passed down from so many parents to their kids: that they should grow up, get married, have children of their own. That doing so would bring them happiness. What ruffled me was the way that he'd expressed it: that all of this—getting married, having kids—was not a choice in life like any other—where to live, what to do, what to devote one's self to—but rather was the only correct path, the thing one *should* be doing.

So many people I know, from the time that they were young, accepted that path without question. Before they were even old enough to think about it, or consider an alternative, they assumed—without examination—that it was not just the thing they'd do, but that it was also what they *wanted* to do. It made me think that we inherit that expectation from our parents. It made me see that getting married and starting a family is a life arrived at, for many, less by volition and more by an assumption they've been carrying all their lives. It made me worry that we internalize that assumption so deeply that we come to believe it is our own desire.

But when I looked at the lives of my friends with kids, I was troubled to find that I didn't see the degree of happiness I thought I was supposed to. Surely it was there—surely it is—but in the day to day, I observed it so rarely. Instead, I saw mostly hurriedness, or harriedness. I saw exhaustion. I saw a desire for solitude, and the rarity of finding it. I saw anxiety. It made this quake of sadness tumble through my chest; it made my heart go out to them.

I'd been quiet, lost in my thoughts while my friends kept talking, but when I snapped back to the present moment it hadn't seemed to matter: Ben was fully horizontal on the porch couch's plush cushions, blinking sleepily at the sway of the lit candle. David was digging deep into a Ziploc bag of Oreos, his eyes happy and half-shut from the weed. Neil had set his beer to the side and was taking careful sips of a mug of tea, and Caesar was buried in his phone, texting his girlfriend back in Mexico City.

"Think I caught a cough on the flight," Neil said apologetically, blowing the steam from the steaming tea. It was clear that they were all ready to sleep.

We wrestled the bag of Oreos away from David, who was stoned and sputtering with laughter, and we piled back into the house. Ben and Caesar were sharing the room with two twin beds, and Neil was given the room with the queen and the private bathroom because, as David said, he was going to be a dad soon, and needed all the sleep he could get, and I tramped down to the basement, where Ben had put my duffel on the foldout bed, upon which Sofia had placed an extra blanket and a cup for water with a little note saying, *In case you get thirsty in the night.* I held it as I read it, touched by the grace and care of this little gesture, my chest filling with something I couldn't quite name.

For some reason I felt near tears. Part of it, I think, was that the note and the feeling it provoked made clear to me how bitter I'd been feeling prior to receiving it: that it was Friday fucking night and my friends just wanted to go to sleep. That I'd been drinking whiskey, and they'd been drinking tea. That I'd driven five hours in a steady heavy rain just to eat a quiet dinner and go to sleep.

But mostly I felt sick at myself, knowing I'd drank too much and would wake diminished, hungover, trying to keep up with my friends when all I'd really desire was quiet and rest. I thought of David climbing into bed with Sofia, Neil texting his wife in Chicago, three months pregnant, telling her good night, Caesar and Ben in their slim twin beds, falling asleep beneath the light of the moon.

As I lay there in the basement feeling that sleep was far from arriving, I thought again about the lives of my friends, the comfort that most of them had found in another person. Even if their happiness wasn't immediately apparent to me, when I looked at my own life it didn't seem full of happiness either: the only thing at its center was myself. I went to bars, I slept with who I wanted, I spent most of my time exactly as I desired. But that relative freedom hadn't yielded the happiness that their lives—from my outside vantage—sometimes seemed to lack. It made me uneasy as I lay there. It made me wonder—and I've wondered more each passing year—whether I had missed a chance, made a choice, and, if so, had it been the wrong one?

The trail for the hike started in a little wooded lot off the side of a two-lane road, and wound its way up into stern spare forest through which could sometimes be seen, in the distance, old stone homes that bordered the public preserve. The climb was steady for a time, but gentle—David's daughter waddled along for a little way before he lifted her into his arms again—and the trail flattened out for long stark stretches where you could look to your left or to your right and see what seemed like forever down the long corridors of forest glimpsed between the slim trees.

As reluctant as I'd been to hike, it did feel good to be outside. The wind hit my face, Ben and Neil tossed a football, Caesar dropped back to talk with Sofia, and I took the quiet as a chance to close my eyes for a few moments, feeling the glow of the cold on my cheeks, the leaves in the blowing wind making a sound like rain.

It had been, as I'd suspected it would be, a struggle to wake up: I hadn't slept well, and I'd stayed in bed listening to breakfast being discussed, then made, then eaten, in the kitchen above me, and then the voices of my friends as they did the dishes, not yet feeling ready in myself, or steady enough, to go upstairs and join them, to try and slide into the rhythm they were already in.

But now the wind and brisk air on the trail were hitting me straight on, and lifting some of the fog that had enveloped me that morning: I felt near to myself, my thoughts clear, my head not aching, something like elation rising inside me at being in the presence of my friends, and at being able to think ahead to the late afternoon, to the particular color the sky would be at 5:00 PM in early November; to mixing drinks, clinking glasses, settling together on the couch, the world outside still visible in the wide gray late-day light.

It was a familiar feeling: hopefulness; something like the fleetingness of life, as someone in a movie might say, but also all its possibility. It brought me back to that day in Michigan. Not the bad parts—the switched timetables, the absent train, the missed audition. I mean before all that: the morning of that day, when we'd hauled the trunk of cold beer down to the beach, and swam together out into the blue, and the unexpected front of warmth that made swimming that day possible. It had been near this very time of year, but years ago: the beginning of November, that day so clear and bright the skyscrapers of Chicago had been visible across the great expanse of the lake.

It's curious, though. From where I write this, what I mostly remember about the morning of the hike is how tired I was. Even within the momentary elation I was feeling, what has remained in time is the fatigue that lay beneath, and that I was attempting to suppress. I was so fucking tired. From here, that's clear to me. I could see the goodness and the glory or whatever you want to call it—the cold of the air, the pack of my friends as they trailed one another through the forest, the beauty of just being there—but it was as if I were seeing it from underneath the sea, and I had a dim awareness that's become clearer in time of how hard I'd have to work to keep up with what seemed to come so easily to everybody else—the conversation, the good spirits, the "esprit de corps" or whatnot. There were so many hours left in the day.

When we got back to the house, I followed behind Ben as we made our way to the small black pond at the edge of David's property. We stripped down to our underwear, then plunged in. It was startling: underneath the water, wrapped in that cold, I decided I'd hold my breath for a little while, but it must have been for longer than I'd thought, because when I finally surfaced, Ben was already out of the pond, trotting back toward the house.

That moment seems, in some ways, an emblem of the rest of the day, or how I felt toward those friends at that time in my life: like I was always behind, anxious to catch up. By the time I toweled off and got up to the house, everyone had showered; by the time I'd showered and gotten dry, Ben was cutting peppers and onions, prepping for dinner, and telling me he didn't need any help. When I finally sat down on the living room couch, the football game I'd wanted to watch was halfway over, and I hurried to pour the afternoon drink I'd hoped for, but when I turned toward the wall of windows looking out onto the garden, the day's last light was gone, the lights in the kitchen were on, and all I could see in the glass was my own reflection.

"G, are we getting after it tonight?"

It was Caesar asking, and suddenly he was behind me, his arms around my chest, and he was lifting me up from the ground in a great heaving bear hug. What he'd meant by his question was "Are we going to get drunk?"

"Duh," I said. "Get those cups," and fifteen minutes later we were smoking cigarettes on the screened-in porch and standing opposite each other as we lofted Ping-Pong balls toward the pyramids of beer-filled cups that were arrayed on our respective sides of the table.

"How are you, babe?" he asked me as we played.

I've never really known how to answer that question. My friends always seemed to say "good," and then share some piece of news from their life, but to say "good" would have felt too simple to me, and I didn't feel I could explain, or even knew, exactly how I was doing. But I said "good" anyway, though all I could think to say as a follow-up was to tell him what happened before I'd left Philadelphia.

The gist of it was that I'd grabbed an alternate baseball cap as I'd rushed to leave my apartment, but with my arms full of the stuff I was bringing to Long Island, I'd placed the cap atop the one I was already wearing, planning to toss it in the trunk when I got to the car. Before getting on the highway toward Long Island, I'd wanted to stop by an all-day reading of that book by James Joyce, *Ulysses*, that was happening at a local church. A local archive and library had recently acquired and was preparing for display a rare edition of the manuscript, and had organized the event in celebration. One of my poli-sci professors had assigned the book in grad school and asked us to read it through the lens of a theory about religion and systems of public good, but I think she simply loved it and wanted an excuse to assign it. I came to love it too, and I slid into one of the church's empty pews as a dim light strained through the panes of stained glass and a man in a bowler hat stood at the microphone, reading from that beautiful scene where Bloom sits in one room of the bar, listening to his friends singing songs in the other, and thinks about his dead son, Rudy, and how much he misses him.

"So here's what happened," I said. "They had kegs of Guinness in the back of the church, so, naturally, I went up to get a glass. The woman pouring was, like, gorgeous. Irish, dark black hair. And Caesar, I swear to God, she kept looking at me and smiling. Like, it was conspicuous—I don't think I was just imagining it. So I pay her for the beer, and I walk back to my seat, and it seems like a couple other people are looking at me too, and all I can think is how I must look *really* good today or something to be getting all this attention.

"I'm smiling ear to ear, drinking beer, listening to people read from this book I love so much, the bartender loves me. Like, what a day. So as I'm sitting there listening, the person reading is reading a passage that describes a guy who's utterly smashed, wearing two of his landlady's hats at once, and as soon as he said 'hat,' I swear to God I audibly gasped. I reached my hand up to my head. I had completely forgotten the second baseball cap was still sitting on top of the first one. I'd been wearing them both that whole time. And I was in that church for like an hour. That's what the woman pouring beer was laughing about. She wasn't smiling at me, she was laughing at me. She must've thought I looked insane."

Caesar was dying at that story, almost howling with laughter. He laughed harder than anyone I knew, and he loved stories like that, where we show ourselves to be as ridiculous as we often are.

"You're the same as you've ever been, Katz," he said when he caught his breath. "You haven't changed at all. It makes me happy."

I know he meant that nicely, but given all that had been in my head the last two days—thinking of my friends' lives in comparison to my own, feeling my own as hazy and uncentered in comparison to theirs—what he said stung me a bit, or brought to the surface the anxiety that had been bubbling underneath since the start of the weekend.

We continued to play. The white balls arced through the air and landed in little splashes in the other person's cups. When I made one of Caesar's, Caesar had to drink all the beer in the cup the ball had landed in, and when he made one of mine, I had to do the same. David came out to smoke a joint while we played, Neil waved from the sloping lawn, where he paced as he spoke on the phone with his wife, and Ben popped his head out to tell us dinner would be ready in ten.

Dinner! Good God! By then we'd had so much beer it seemed unlikely I was going to eat much, but I split a quick cigarette with Caesar and we trudged into the dining room, where I was relieved to see an open bottle of wine on the table, hoping to continue the fun.

Then everyone was sitting down, passing around a platter heaped with roasted chicken pulled from the bone, trading that for steaming bowls of Spanish rice, guacamole, warm tortillas, and a roasting pan full of a mound of spiced peppers. We dined. I poured wine for everyone who wanted it, and listened as David and Sofia mentioned the trouble they were having trying to get their daughter enrolled into a decent preschool.

"Wait, isn't she like, barely two years old?" I asked.

Everyone laughed, but I saw my question had come off as more derisive than I'd meant.

"I just mean—how early do kids go to school? That seems crazy that you'd even have to be thinking about that right now."

"It is crazy," David said. "But it's fucking private school in New Haven and like insanely competitive to get your kids into what people think are the 'right' preschools. The parents are crazy. I mean, so are we. But yeah, people's thinking is that if they don't get their kid into the right preschool, they won't get into the right grade school, which means the wrong high school, which means a mediocre college, which means a mediocre life, the way they think about it."

"Mhm," I said, swallowing some wine as I nodded that I understood. "That sounds fucking miserable."

"I mean, it is," said Sofia, "but also it makes sense, you know? It's not ideal but it's the environment we're in, and there's some truth to it."

"Truth to what?" I asked. "That if a kid doesn't get into an Ivy League preschool they'll end up at, I don't know, God forbid, the University of Nebraska?"

I was kidding about Nebraska, but it was a mean thing to say, for a couple of reasons. One: Neil had gone there, and in mentioning it I had unfairly suggested Sofia thought it was a shitty school. Two: it was the most ungenerous interpretation of what she'd meant. She had no problem with Nebraska. In reality it probably wasn't exactly where she envisioned her kid going, but what was wrong with that? She just wanted the best life for her kid, as anyone would.

"No, obviously there's nothing wrong with Nebraska." She laughed. "You know, except for the fact that Neil went there," she said, winking at him across the table.

She was so good at doing that: defusing a tense situation by making people laugh, putting forward the same assertion that I had accused her of but as a joke, and in doing so gently showing Neil there was no part of her heart that felt that way.

"No. The truth," she continued, "is that where you go to school matters. I mean, look at all of you. I mean, come on—you all went to one of the best private high schools in Chicago. You're telling me you wouldn't do everything you could to give your kid that same opportunity?"

It was a fair point. More than fair. She was right. But in that moment, having drunk as much as I had, I saw that she'd gotten, already, the better of me, and I didn't want to agree.

"I'm not so sure I would," I said. "Send my kids there, I mean. If I had them. I mean if I ever have them."

And suddenly my own age didn't seem young to me at all. I was thirty-one years old that day, and the prospect of kids, of even meeting someone who I might one day want to have them with, and who might want to have them with me, seemed, in that moment, very improbable.

I doubled down.

"I don't really think I would," I said.

"Why not?" asked Sofia.

"I don't know," I said. "I think it's the uniformity I have an issue with. Rich kids, mostly white. Everyone with the same politics as their parents, the same snobbishness. People's parents at our school, like, genuinely scared me in how intense they were about their kids' futures."

Sofia snorted into the glass of orange juice she was drinking.

"Graham, kids don't have political beliefs. Like, I'm not going to purposefully send my kid to a shittier school just so they can be 'exposed to a variety of people and viewpoints.' They have the whole rest of their lives for that."

I almost laugh to remember that, how cutting it was when she said it, though I could see her point. I almost started to argue anyway, but there was something else, too, suddenly swimming in my head, a memory of Sam that felt connected to what I was trying to say. Sam had been suspended. I had almost forgotten that. My senior year of high school.

She'd shown up drunk to the Pageant of the Twelve Days (that yearly Christmas pageant where, as freshmen, we'd sat there, utterly stunned, for the first time watching Jana dance). We all were drunk, but Sam was tiny and had overdone it, and a teacher walked in to find her and three other girls from her class singing in the bathroom, absolutely hammered, pretending the cardboard from a roll of toilet paper was a microphone.

Sam received a week's suspension while the other girls were only punished with after-school tutorial, meaning their record was clean where Sam's was not. It infuriates me to remember. The only difference between Sam and the three girls was that they had rich parents who the school administration was scared of, whereas Sam's mom could hardly get out of bed. All of them had done the exact same thing, but Sam was the only one to get suspended. I explained that at the dinner table. Schools like the one we went to didn't treat people the same. Something similar had happened to Ryan.

And now I asked about him. How was he?

"Fine, I think," said Neil. "I texted with him recently. He's living in Ohio. He got married. Still working as a recruiter for the marines."

And what about Jana? There was silence in response. I looked around the table, and everyone just shrugged.

"Why are you guys so quiet?" I asked. "She didn't, like, die or something, did she?"

Someone laughed, "No, not as far as I know."

"You guys aren't curious?" I asked.

"About what?" said Ben.

"About how she is."

"Sure," he said, "a little bit," but he shrugged his shoulders. "Not more than I am about anyone else we went to high school with, I suppose. Why should I be?"

I was surprised by his flippancy.

"I kind of think we all should be," I said. I thought the reason why would be obvious to them. I looked at their faces for some sign of agreement.

"All of us should be curious," I said. "We're the reason she and Ryan aren't together."

David scoffed.

"How are we responsible for that?"

"We are literally the reason he missed her audition."

Ben laughed.

"That's not the only reason they broke up," he said.

I disagreed.

"If he hadn't missed it," I said, "she never would've broken up with him."

"Ryan's an alcoholic," David interjected. He said it in a sighing, exasperated way, as though it explained everything. "I know he's not drinking now but he was back then, and I'm sure that was not the worst thing he'd ever done to her. And anyway," he said, "why does it matter? We were in high school. None of that was that serious, none of it would have lasted. Think of anyone you were with back then."

I did. I thought not of Sam but immediately of Nina, college, Spring Fling, the weekend she and I had spent together with Casey and Molly in Palm Springs. I thought of her paintings, their lonely pale shapes of people, the last time that I had seen her: it had been the winter after I'd left Los Angeles for good. She'd finished college but stayed in Southern California. She painted during the day and worked most evenings as a hostess at the restaurant of a fancy hotel in LA. I had dropped out of grad school by then, and was living in Chicago. Even though we'd broken up, we'd stayed in touch. I went back to see her in LA.

I remember the bus ride from the airport, visiting Nina at her studio, wanting so badly to sleep with her right there on the studio's cement floor I could hardly speak. I was lonely, and I desired her. But had I desired her solely because I was lonely? Or had my desire been a sign of something more?

I'd stood close beside her, examining a painting she had made, our breath slowing until it fell into the same rhythm.

"You still have a bed in here," I said, pointing to the blankets piled beneath the worktable, the space where she'd sometimes sleep if it became too late to catch the bus.

But in the end, I couldn't even find the courage to try and take her hand. I just stood there beside her, looking at her paintings, my shoulder nearly touching hers, but not. She closed up her studio. We waited in the twilight for the bus. We grew quiet. I left the next morning. I hadn't seen or spoken to her since.

Ryan's an alcoholic. David's words were ringing in my head. The way he'd said it ruffled something in me. It seemed so final, indicting, like a fact that made Ryan a lost cause. I thought again of the email from Sam he'd forwarded to all our friends. I was being harsh, but there was something in that action that felt like it overlapped with his dismissiveness toward Ryan, as if he wanted to scrub anything unpleasant from his life, or make fun of it.

That wasn't a fair accusation on my part, and somewhere in my heart I knew it, but in that moment I didn't care. I thought of Sam, the wealth I was surrounded by, the utter security of it. I thought about the utter security of all our lives in comparison to hers.

My friends had never been very kind to her. Not to me, either, in the time that I was with her. She hadn't fit in easily with them. Her father was absent; her mother was sick with mental illness, shut up in her bedroom, sometimes for days on end. I'd seen her scream at Sam once when Sam knocked to ask if she could have some money for lunch. It had stunned me. My heart froze to see that unprovoked meanness, but it gave me a clearer understanding of Sam and the black hole of her life at home. It made me see what had previously been invisible to me: what an effort it must have been for her to go to school each day, to laugh along at the jokes her friends made, to be a person who could seem like everything was okay. Perhaps my friends, back then, had sensed that well of pain in her, and wanted nothing to do with it. Whatever it was that provoked their coldness toward her, they had made their feelings known. They'd left us out of their plans. If they were on their way somewhere and saw us coming, they turned away.

"Anyway," David said, interrupting my thoughts, steering the conversation back to his and Sofia's search for a preschool, wanting to defuse the tension. "Sof and I at least have some good advisors in the school department."

"Wait, like who?" she asked.

"Mark and Layla," David answered, then he turned to us to explain: "They're a couple we met at the playground—not here, but back in New Haven."

"They've got a newborn and a three-year-old boy," said Sofia. "We see them literally every time we're at the playground. Mark and Layla are dealing with the same school stress that we are, and their boy is obsessed with Addy, apparently—Mark always jokes that we're going to have no choice but to send them to the same school."

"Yeahhhh, we're not doing that though," David interjected. He was laughing, but you could tell he was serious.

"What do you mean?" I asked.

"Nothing, nothing," he said, waving his hands. "Just that we're not sending Addy to the same school as their son."

"We're not really trying to encourage that relationship," added Sofia.

"Why not?" I asked

"Why not what?" said Sofia.

"Why are you guys trying to not encourage that relationship?"

"Well," Sofia said. She looked over at David.

"The general consensus is that their son seems . . . kind of dumb?" David said, laughing.

I opened my mouth to say something but Sofia interjected.

"Anyway, it's a mess," she said. "It's competitive. It's a headache. That's sort of how it goes with private schools in New Haven, I guess," she said, and shrugged. "It'll work out."

"Making friends with parents at the playground," Caesar joked. "You guys are really aging fast."

"Sof gives me shit about it," said David. "Says I don't try hard enough with other parents."

"You don't, my love," she said.

"It's true," David said. "But, like, I already have friends! I don't particularly want new ones! And all the other parents want to talk about is preschool and neighborhood gossip."

"That sounds . . . bitchy and awful," I said.

"The parents we've met are really not so bad," said Sofia.

"They sound like it," I said.

"What makes you say that?" asked Sofia.

"Well, weren't you guys just telling me you didn't want Addy spending time with someone else's son because he's too dumb?"

There was a silence for a second in which some unfolding calculation was taking place inside my head about the words that I had just said, and it was steadily coming clear to me that in effect, inadvertently, they'd added up to me leveling a hatchet at them both. I felt sick with myself. That had not been my intention. I had meant to push back on what seemed like a thoughtless comment on their end, but I hadn't wanted to sound cruel. I was trying, in a broader sense, to push against the general craziness in how we raise our kids: as if we could, that early on, tether them to a future of our choosing; as if we had volition over that; as if we would even want to.

But the words had come out as they had, and my mind went white recognizing what I'd implied and how desperately I wished I could unsay it, and the impossibility of that.

Sofia cleared her throat a little, but didn't say anything.

"That just sounds like a tough environment," I stammered, trying to cover up what I'd said. "I mean, I feel for you—it must be really stressful and I obviously know you guys only want good things for Addy. It's just wild to me that that planning has to start so early."

My throat was thick and in my heart I wanted to cry, hearing how shallow my words sounded in the wake of what I'd said, but all I could do was swallow hard, trying to suppress the shame and sadness rising in my chest.

Many nights I have lain sleepless in a darkened room, as I did that night, thinking about my life, and how it's always seemed to me that in moments of greatest need, or despair, when I was stuck in a dilemma I wasn't able to see a way out of, or beset by worry, something arrived that showed me a way forward, something that Sam, in the vocabulary of her AA meetings, might've called "grace," and in time these arrivals have given me the belief that there is a presence beyond us to which we can appeal for help. Does it seem that way to you?

The next morning I woke up early, consumed by regret. David and Sofia, with Sofia carrying Addy in her arms, came downstairs to find me at the dining room table. They were surprised I was already awake.

"Coffee?" David asked, then made some for all of us, then he and Sofia sat down beside me.

"I'm glad you're up so early," said David.

He said they'd been wanting to find a time to talk to me privately that weekend, away from everyone else.

"You're one of our oldest friends," Sofia said.

And then, in the warm room, in the light of the morning, with the trees and woods of Long Island outside the windows, dark against the white November sky, while everyone else was sleeping, they asked me if, when he arrived, I would be willing to be the godfather to their son.

I said yes.

I said, "Yes, yes, of course I will." I laid my face in my hands and I wept.

Ohio

And that's just how it happens: one year had slipped into five (college was over, Ryan would soon be home from Afghanistan), five years had slipped into seven (I'd begun graduate school in Los Angeles), seven years became seven more (David had two kids, Neil had one, Donald Trump was our president, and Ryan was living in Ohio), then fifteen became sixteen, sixteen became seventeen, and by then the years since I'd seen or spoken to Ryan were greater than the years I'd known him.

I was astonished to discover that fact. I was lying in bed in a motel room in Columbus, Ohio, very very early on a freezing Sunday morning, counting the years on my fingers. I was there for the weekend for the wedding of a friend, and I woke that day knowing in my heart that I needed to go see Ryan, or at least to try.

I had driven from Philadelphia to Columbus for the wedding, and I had a window to see Ryan that was conveniently brief—late that morning or not at all—before beginning the long drive home. I had to be at work on Monday, and the fixed deadline gave me courage. I'd woken Sunday morning thinking of Ryan, and with my thoughts came a terrible dread inside my chest. He'd either be able to see me or, hopefully, not, but I knew when I woke that I had to call him. It's hard to describe exactly why, but not to do so seemed, that morning, like it would have been an irrevocable sin, one that I wouldn't be able to forgive myself for.

I had been thinking, of course, of the timetables we'd switched in Michigan, the absent train, Ryan missing Jana's audition, and the way those events had altered his life. I felt—and perhaps it was my state of mind—raw eyed and hungover, tired from travel and lack of sleep—that I was being given a chance to make amends, to call him out of the blue, to see him, and, maybe, even to own up to what we'd done. I felt, in that state, that I was being put to a test by something beyond me, and not to take it would be a turning away, a decision I feared would be a weight upon me for the rest of my life.

Ryan had been on my mind. On my way to Columbus, I'd passed a sign in western Pennsylvania for the Flight 93 Memorial. I hadn't thought about that plane in years, and hadn't realized the crash site was in the same state in which I lived. And the week before the trip, I'd texted my friends about the wedding, and told them where it was.

Ryan's neck of the woods, Neil responded, and when I'd read that I felt my chest close tight around my heart. Stars I didn't want to align seemed to be aligning. Neil said Ryan was living outside Columbus with his wife and daughter. It would be a quick drive from where I was staying.

Central Ohio in late January, gray and cold. I had called; Ryan had answered; and now he was walking toward the diner door as I pulled into the lot, dropping the last of his cigarette into the slush. His truck was silver, caked at the back with blackish snow, like the winter ground of Ohio had climbed aboard, trying to reclaim it.

"Ryan!" I called from my open window. He turned on his heels, his hands jammed into the pockets of his coat, and threw his head back in fake surprise when he caught sight of me. He trudged over, his head bent against the biting wind. We slapped hands through the open window, and I used both of mine to hold on to his for an extra beat, trying to communicate a warmth, trying to tell him that I was truly glad to see him.

"Graham fucking Katz," he said. "Park. I'll get us a table."

Ryan had thrived in the marines. I'd had a peripheral sense of that fact from the occasional updates I'd get from Neil, and from what Caesar had told me about him getting sober over there, but it became even clearer as we talked what a pivotal structure the marines had been for him. When his deployment was over, he'd started working for them as a recruiter, traveling around the country—Fresno, Charleston, El Paso—wherever they needed him—working the booth at street festivals or career fairs on weekends, then running trainings at the MCRDs in San Diego or Parris Island during the week.

He told me this over breakfast. He and his wife, Leah (he called her "Lee"), were living outside Columbus. When Lee got pregnant, so as to travel less, Ryan had switched to a new job with the marines, administering the required intelligence test to would-be recruits in central and western Ohio.

How was life?

"Ah," he said, and stopped. "Uh, complicated. A little stressful."

He wasn't kidding. He and Lee had two kids: a teenager from Lee's earlier marriage and five-year-old Cleo, who they'd had together. Cleo was nonverbal.

"Verbal apraxia," Ryan said. He was smoothing out the paper place mat with his hands, adjusting the bottom until it was in perfect alignment with the lip of the table.

"It took us a long time to figure it out. They thought at first she was just coming slow to language. We hoped so badly that was true. But when Cleo turned four and still wasn't forming words, they started saying with more certainty it was apraxia. In between was kind of a nightmare. The doctors told us all sorts of things—that it could be autism, maybe, or ADHD. Lee and I wanted badly to believe that's what it was. It wouldn't have been as hard a road for Cleo."

He kept his eyes on the place mat as he spoke. As I listened to him, I could only think that he seemed softer. I couldn't exactly put my finger on it at the time, but he'd grown more gentle, I sensed, or more calm. There was so much less of the manic edge to him that had been there when we were young. He seemed centered, his breathing slow and even, his big hands resting on the table between us.

I was kind of moved to see that calmness in him when it was so incongruous with the Ryan I remembered as a teenager. But I also found it jarring in a way, or melancholy, like that movie where a boy encounters in a zoo the dragon he'd once known as a fierce free creature. The boy loops his hands through the thick metal bars of the dragon's cage. He beckons his old friend close. He leans his head against the dragon's own. He weeps at its newfound quiet, for the way that it's been tamed, for what he believes the dragon has lost; and he weeps for himself, because the dragon before him is no longer the dragon he had known.

Ryan talked about his job, his wife and kids, his life in Columbus. In the little free time that he had, he was helping Afghan refugees around Columbus find permanent housing, at least the ones who wanted it.

For a second I didn't understand, and then I did. The people he was helping were people who'd had to flee when the Taliban retook Kabul in the wake of the sudden withdrawal of nearly all our troops in 2021. Some of them were Afghans who had worked as translators for the US military. Some of them families of people who'd assisted the US in some way. In a lot of instances, he said, the family member who'd actually provided help to Americans never made it out, they were captured or killed after the US troops left. In a single day, with the Taliban spreading through the city again, they'd gone from being assured a future by their American employers to being labeled traitors by the Taliban troops that were flooding Kabul's streets.

I remembered that time. I'd been driving back to Philadelphia from Virginia. I'd spent the night in Richmond, where I'd gotten drunk at a bar and made conversation with a young server wearing a big brass peace sign as a necklace. She was living in a van, trying to find a way out of Richmond. I got so drunk I thought I was in love and wrote my number and a comically long note on the back of the check, and—unsurprisingly—never heard from her. The next morning, hungover and exhausted, driving out of the city through the brutal Virginia heat, I'd turned the radio on and started to hear the first reports of the US, seemingly overnight, fleeing Afghanistan. The Taliban were coming out of the mountains. They were taking one town, then another, more or less without resistance. The US-backed Afghan military was putting down its arms. The reporter was describing those awful scenes I later saw on television: people clinging to the wings of the departing planes. I mentioned that memory to Ryan.

"Yeah," he said. "I'd be lying if I said that this was my original intention, to get so deeply involved with all that." He meant the volunteer work he was doing with the refugees; he'd been doing it now for just over a year. "They know I'm military. They're suspicious of me," he said. "I don't blame them. But I know it's the right thing that I'm there, 'a good deed' and all that shit. It's what they say in AA. 'Just work the program, and it will work for you.' And mostly it does. So I do it.

"I was just so fucking angry when we left. At the way we did. What a fucking stab in the back," he said. "What a fucking betrayal. Sorry," he said, "with the language. I just still get heated about it. Twenty fucking years down the drain in a day.

"I didn't know what to do," he continued. "I didn't know what I was going to do."

Then he told me a story. When his wife went to work one day, during the period of the withdrawal, he was left there just slouching on the couch, watching the news. They were showing those videos I mentioned, of people so desperate to flee the Taliban they attached themselves to departing planes. The videos showed them being blown off the wings, dropping back to earth, their bodies skidding along the tarmac, cartwheeling across it like a race car smashing into a wall then flipping across a track.

Ryan told me he drove, that day, to the VA Vet Center. He parked in the parking lot. He sat out there in the sun, looking toward the sliding glass doors of the entrance.

"Obviously it made no fucking sense," he said. "The VA didn't have anything to do with how we left Afghanistan. And it's the Nam guys who really hate the VA, not the ought-three and Afghanistan guys."

I looked at him questioningly.

"Ought-three," he said. "Zero three. Two thousand and three. The year we invaded Iraq. But yeah, it's the old guys who have a problem with the VA. Twenty-first-century guys just kill ourselves or kill our girlfriends."

He waited for me to laugh.

I didn't.

"I'm kidding," he said. "Anyway, my problem was with Joe Biden and the dumb fucks who drew up the withdrawal like that, but Biden doesn't take my calls and I live in fucking Ohio, so the VA was the only place I could think to drive to."

Ryan stopped.

"Don't really know why I'm telling you this. I didn't tell Lee, probably won't ever tell Moonie or Val or anyone I was over there with. Probably telling you 'cause you're basically a stranger, so what does it matter."

Stranger. It stung me to hear that he saw me as such, though I saw that it was true.

"I wasn't going to, like, *do* something," he continued, "certainly not to someone else. I was just kind of sitting there. I got tired. I almost fell asleep."

I tried to picture him there: drowsy in the afternoon heat, checking his phone, watching the minutes pass. I imagined him closing his eyes, trying to make his breathing steady. He told me he started thinking about his sobriety. He thought of his wife, he said. He thought about his life.

"I was so angry," Ryan said. "I was shaking—my hands were when I looked at them. The rage I felt that day. I don't know. It made me get those PETA people or whatever—throwing blood on furs. It made me get how people come to give their life to protest. Or take their life, I guess. You know what I mean? Like that guy in Chicago who killed himself on the side of the highway against Iraq? In protest? Fuck," he said, shaking his head to remember.

"But also the climate people—gluing themselves to opera seats and shit while they scream their heads off about fossil fuels—it made that make more sense to me. Like, they're screaming because they can't believe that all of us aren't. We all must seem insane to them for just living our lives like normal."

Ryan told me he'd sat there through the whole afternoon, then into the evening. He watched employees file out into the dusk. One would come out, get into their car, start the engine, drive away. A few minutes would pass, then another person would exit. He sat there for a long time. He watched the lot grow empty.

"And then this guy comes out," Ryan told me. "By that time mine and his are like the only two cars in the parking lot, and this guy looks around for a minute, looks over at my truck, and then starts walking straight toward my car, kind of waving as he comes, like he's trying to flag me down or something.

"And my blood is just fucking boiling. I'm thinking he's coming over to ask me what I'm doing there, to kick me out, like he's security or something. My blood pressure's at, like, nine hundred as he gets near the truck. I'm ready to get into it. I'm ready to fucking fight. And I've got this whole script going in my head, a whole crazy dialogue about how things were about to go, how he's gonna ask me what I'm doing there or tell me to move, and how I'm about to tell him it's a free fucking country and I'll park wherever the fuck I'd like."

"So what happened?" I asked.

"A bird was stuck in the stairwell."

"What?" I laughed. "What do you mean?"

"I mean that's what he came over for," Ryan said. "Why he came over to talk to me. He said there's this bird that had gotten past the sliding doors and got itself trapped in the stairwell. He asked for my help. He said everyone had left and he wanted me to help him catch this bird. It caught me so off guard I didn't know what to do but say yes.

"So I just get out of the truck and trudge up with him to the fucking VA, and we spend the next, like, forty minutes trying to trap this little fucking bird without killing it. I mean it was insane. He gives me this broom and I'm holding it in the air, waving it at the bird, trying to scare it down; the bird is, like, smashing itself against the stairwell window, and the guy is standing on the steps below with an empty wastebasket to trap it once we get it down, and meanwhile he's, like, screaming at me about my technique, or whatever. I was about ready to murder him. He was telling me I need to shimmy the bird to the ceiling corner or something; the bird is going apeshit, a robin or something, I don't know; it was so tiny I thought for sure he was gonna crush it on accident with the edge of that waste can if we ever even managed to get it to the ground.

"Didn't though. I mean didn't crush it. We got it to the ground, finally, and clamped the can down over it to trap it. It made a fucking racket once it was in there, but we slipped some cardboard underneath so the top would be covered when we flipped it over, and then we, like, wobbled to the front door as fast as we could to free it. We must have looked crazy. He's holding the trash can out in front of him like you'd carry a dog out of the house as it's already pissing, and I'm running alongside with my hand clamped down on the cardboard to keep the bird from busting through before we get outside, and when we finally do we plop the can down on the asphalt, pull the cardboard off, and it just shot out of there back into the sky."

I realized I'd almost been holding my breath as he'd been telling that story, and took a long drink of water.

"That was sort of that," Ryan said. "The guy asked if I was okay. I said, 'I'm okay.' He gave me his card. He drove away.

"It was strange. The thing with the bird really caught me sideways. I'd been so angry all day, but then it was gone."

I made a little noise of recognition, just a sound in my throat.

"And then you left?" I asked.

"I called my wife."

He'd called her, and told her that he'd gone for a drive, that he'd been thinking of her, and that he'd called just because he wanted to say hello.

"And then she goes, 'Is everything alright?'"

Ryan laughed as he told me that. "That call was so out of character for me that Lee actually asked me if everything was okay. She was suspicious. She thought I was feeling guilty about something. I guess I must never call her, at least for no reason. I was being so nice she thought something must be wrong."

I got the impression that Ryan and Lee were having a hard time of things.

"It's constant," he said. "We're exhausted. This country doesn't make it very easy for people with disabilities. I mean, this country doesn't make it easy to take care of *anyone* who needs care, really. Cleo's kindergarten basically kicked her out. Like, legally, they can't, but they said she wouldn't ever get from them the support she needs. 'No budget, no resources,' whatever. All that shit. You can imagine. They just threw up their hands. But yeah—a lot gets put onto me and Lee, and most of the time I feel like we're so busy with care for Cleo that we don't even look at each other."

Ryan's current job with the marines was essentially an administrative position. He'd stand at the front of the classroom and read the test instructions to the kids who wanted to enlist, then sit at the desk while they took the test. It was a good job, he said.

"Boring as fuck but I'm not going to complain."

The pay was good. The job was easy. He said he had ways to help the kids pass the intelligence test, the ones he knew wouldn't be able to pass on their own.

I raised an eyebrow. He shrugged his shoulders.

"It's a lifeline for a lot of them," he said. "I'm gonna tell them they're not even smart enough to join the fucking military? Everyone in their life is telling them they're not smart enough. That's why they're in that room with me in the first place. Let them get to basic. If it doesn't work out from there it doesn't work out, but they at least deserve a shot."

Outside, the gray day was trying to come alive, but it was undercut by the endless steel shelf of sky. Cars were filling the lot; the bell above the diner door kept dinging each time the door opened; people stamped their feet in the vestibule near the front, blowing heat into their cold hands, waiting for a table.

I reached for the check, but Ryan slid it from my reach, then went up to the counter to pay. The lady making change laughed at something he said. As he stood there, I looked at him. I looked at his boots. They were true work boots, a light-tan leather, bruised from use, the leather blackened in spots from water or wear, and there was a little silver ball hanging down from one of the lace holes, like a dangly silver earring.

He laughed when I asked.

"It's a bell," he explained, coming back with the change. "Cleo's got one too. She made me tie it to her shoe, then went and got my boot, and she screamed her head off until I tied one to my own."

Sometimes I think how anything, everything, in each moment of our lives, is available to us, if we only have the courage to say the thing in our mind. I think about how, sitting there before another person, we have the opportunity to say anything at all. You might be in a crowded shop on a Saturday, and the person you are with is admiring the shape of the glass she's holding in her hands, and you could say, "I want to go home with you, I want to go to bed with you." Or she might be telling you about the hike she took the day before and how her feet got so muddy it was unbelievable, and you could take her hand and say, "My love, some days I miss my mom so much it scares me."

Sometimes I think about what that would cost: speaking openly, expressing what we feel. Hardly anything, it seems. We spend almost every single second of our lives letting the seconds pass us by, not saying the things we think, not asking the questions in our mind, not admitting to the desires we might have. Why?

On the table before us, Ryan arranged the little empty cups of cream into a wavering line. *I'm sorry for what we did, and I'm sorry for our absence*, is what I wanted to say, but failed to. *I love you*, is what I wish I'd said. *I hope you know that.*

As Ryan reached for his wallet to show me a picture of Cleo, I had to turn my head to the side; I had to pretend to look at the world outside for a moment while I tried to tamp down the sadness filling my chest. It wasn't because Ryan seemed unhappy. He was animated; he was as steady as I'd ever seen him; he'd told me he'd bought Cleo a xylophone and thought sometimes that that was how they spoke—through the rhythms she'd make on the long wooden keys and the ones he'd make to answer, in a call and response.

No, I was sad because of all the things I'd have liked to say and didn't, and because I felt I understood, sitting there with him, that Ryan's life would be hard. I don't mean to say his situation was tragic or impossible—I don't think it's for anyone to say what someone else's life is. But it seemed like life was never going to be easy for him, that it kept presenting one hardship after another, and I worried about how tired he might become.

We stepped out into the lot.

Jesus Christ it was gray outside. It was so fucking gray.

On the two-lane highway, cars sped by us, their headlights on though it was only 12:00 PM, as if they knew something was coming that we did not, and were hurrying to get home.

It's hard to say exactly why, but it put a fear in me. The dark gray of the day; time speeding by. It was only early afternoon, but it felt like evening. I felt I needed to say something meaningful. I wanted to say something that would make Ryan feel that I really saw him and understood him. I don't know why I felt the need to do that, or why I thought he needed that from me. But when I thought of saying a normal goodbye, just slapping hands as we had that night in the parking lot behind my parents' house, many many years ago, it didn't seem right, or it felt like it would be incomplete.

During breakfast, Ryan had asked how I was doing, what I'd been up to, and I'd tried to give him a snapshot: my life in Philadelphia, my job at the nonprofit, the winding way I got there;

how I'd been in grad school in Los Angeles for a public policy program, and then—I'd admitted a little sheepishly—how I'd left the program before I'd finished.

Ryan had listened as I spoke. He said it all sounded good to him, then took the conversation elsewhere, for which I was grateful. Most people in my life, when I told them I'd dropped out, tended to respond very gingerly. I could tell they wanted to know what happened that led me not to finish but didn't want to ask outright, assuming, maybe, that it was something I was ashamed of. Or maybe they themselves were ashamed for me.

What are you up to? It was a conversation I'd had a thousand times with other friends and family; one that so often got weighed down with further queries I didn't have the answer to—*why was I interested in this particular field, what was I going to do next, what was the end goal*—whereas Ryan didn't ask what the job was in service of, what I hoped it would lead to, as if everything had to be a stepping stone on a path to something more. He just shrugged and said, "Cool," and accepted what it was.

Now I wanted him to think, in some perverse reversal of the sense I'd always had that he could see me clearly, or see clearly through the person I presented myself to be, that I really saw him, or at least that I'd heard him.

"I think what you're doing is a good thing," I managed to stammer. "I mean working with the refugees, even helping recruit those kids for the marines." I was thinking of Sam too, and the way, as I saw it, he'd saved her life.

"I feel like that work doesn't always get noticed, but I think you're making a difference in people's lives," I said. "Even if you don't see it in the immediate term, I think the way you show up for them now is going to bring real long-term good to them."

Ryan was standing beside my car. He was smoking a cigarette, and his eyes were looking at the ground as I spoke. He was nudging a mound of slush back and forth against my driver's side wheel, and even before I could finish speaking he was nodding his head and saying, "Thanks man, thanks, I appreciate that," but it felt to me as if my words embarrassed him, and he was hurrying me to get them over with.

"You got a second?" he said. "I want to show you something."

"Sure." I looked at my watch. It was 12:11 PM. Philadelphia—home—seemed so far away. I felt I really needed to get going.

He pointed back toward the diner, then motioned for me to follow him. He led me around the side of it, past a row of grit-caked windows looking into the diner kitchen, then out to the diner's backside.

We were on a hill, I realized. You wouldn't have been able to tell from the front, but the diner was perched at the hill's flat top. From where we stood, we looked out onto the depths of a valley that stretched out before us, the low sky hovering over it, an unbroken gray that went as far as we could see. It was a beautiful view.

"Do you believe in climate change?" Ryan asked.

I laughed.

"Yes," I said.

"Good," he said. "Me too." He paused. "See what they're building there?"

Down in the valley, motionless yellow construction vehicles sat parked beside mounds of earth the size of small hills, which themselves stood dwarfed by the rebar and cinder-block frames of a sequence of massive rectangular structures rising from the valley floor.

"That's going to be a new shipping warehouse. People are excited about it. One hundred thousand jobs. You can order any item in the world and when this is up and running they'll be able to get it to you in under six hours."

I wasn't really following.

"Here's the thing," he continued. "The great disaster all these scientists keep telling us is going to come if we don't do something? It's already arrived. It's already here. They say we can still stop it, but we can't. I'm a little nervous."

I made a noise of assent, though in truth I wasn't really sure what he was getting at.

"What are you nervous about?" I asked.

"A lot," he replied. "Climate change. This fucking country. People's minds. What's going to happen to my daughter when I die.

"Think of the biggest, darkest wave in the ocean. I mean a horror-movie-level wave: so high and ferocious, so big and wide it seems like it came from another planet. No one can see it, but that's what we're standing underneath. And when it breaks, let me tell you. All of this," he said, gesturing toward the construction site, then more generally to the world around us, "this is all going to unravel faster than anyone can imagine, and it's going to get very fucking dark. January 6 was a glimpse, but that doesn't even come close. Do you know how many guns there are in this country? Four hundred million. Do you know the people who own most of them? You don't. You probably don't want to. And I hope that you don't come to find out. But this is a delusion," he said, nodding toward the silent diggers and the skeletal frames of the unbuilt buildings. "I'm afraid people are going to come to understand that in a way they won't forget."

That was what Ryan left me with.

Jesus, I thought, as I drove toward Philadelphia, but I also couldn't stop thinking about his words. They frightened me. They reminded me, in their tenor and warning and in what they tapped into, of a feeling that had crept into me those first couple years after the 2016 election, right about the time I'd convened at Riverhead with all the guys, when David and Sofia asked me to be the godfather to their son. I'd been worried, at that time; maybe even more than worried. I'd looked around me and felt fearful at the things I saw: the vitriol coming from the Capitol; the blunt refusal by President Trump and the rest of his administration to admit to or acknowledge objective reality; and the increasingly frightening willingness on the part of his supporters to insist that what they knew not to be true was true.

There'd been a film that came out in the summer of 2016 that wasn't ostensibly related to politics at all, but the plot of which gave me chills. It posited a reality in which on one night each year, as a means of population management or getting rid of "undesirables," everyone would be allowed to kill whoever they wished without fear of legal repercussion. It was the summer before the election, Donald Trump was named the Republican nominee just a few weeks after the film's release, and the movie seemed, in that climate, a dangerous line of thought to put into the world, even if it billed itself as unrealistic horror, because I worried that to certain supporters of his, that idea wouldn't seem unreasonable, or far-fetched.

And then he got elected. Sometimes, during those years of his presidency, unable to sleep, I'd read the message boards of the MAGA camp. What I saw there scared me, particularly as the 2020 election grew nearer. It put in me a growing certainty that even if President Trump were to lose, he wouldn't simply give up office. I couldn't have put into words at that time the exact nature of what I feared might happen, but as the radio reports began to come in on January 6 of mobs of his supporters storming the Capitol, I saw that what I'd feared was coming true. That siege came, I believe, a few months too late to have had any chance at succeeding, but the ferocity of that day, the willingness of the people in that crowd to kill, and the righteousness they professed in doing so, left me frightened, and that fear has never left. That's what Ryan's words that day in Ohio made me think of. As I drove I turned them over, and believed that he had seen the same thing I did and, like myself, feared—and perhaps anticipated—that something worse might be on its way.

Two hours past Wheeling I began to see the signs on the side of the highway for the Flight 93 Memorial. It was almost 4:00 PM. When I neared Somerset I took the ramp to my right, exiting the interstate, and I followed the signs along the road winding through hills and farmland, pointing me in the direction of the visitor center.

It was pretty barren out there. I was only a handful of miles from the interstate, but the stripped hills and the diminishing light of Sunday evening made me feel far away from everything. When I got there, I exited the car and looked out, first back toward the highway, and then down the path to the Tower of Voices, a pillar of hollow stone rising gray and jagged atop a bare hill, like it was the last standing remnant of an ancient temple.

The barrenness made me think. I guess it should've been obvious, but somehow the bare fact of the earth around me—the fields and forest on either side stretching as far as you could see—made clear to me that before the crash those particular acres of Pennsylvania land had been simply what they'd been, miles of grassland and forest, cold creeks with boulders in their middle that had sat there—their patient faces washed by the flowing water—for millions of years. Now the area was a pilgrimage site for people wanting to remember the strange event that had unfolded in the sky above that hillside; people there to mourn, some of them, the lives that had been lost, while others came just because they had happened to notice the sign for it on the highway, and wanted to see.

Thinking of that tower now, it seems so sad and ramshackle. Pipes hung inside the stone tower's hollow middle—one for each life lost in the crash—and knocked against the others when the wind passed through them to make a sound like music. I stood beneath them for a while, looking up, then walked in a circle around the tower. A small placard said the chimes had been installed and the site commemorated in September 2020, but that was nineteen years after the fact of the event. All that time it took before the tower was built filled me with a feeling I couldn't quite name. The chimes hung in the air, dangling from their strings like salamis, or bodies, swaying without sound in the cold wind of early evening. The sun was nearly setting. You could see clear across that landscape, the middle of Pennsylvania, hardly anything around me, and something about the light and the hour turned everything suddenly sad, or lonely.

Have you ever read the transcripts from September 11 of people's last phone calls? People on the hijacked planes, people in the towers? I read them once; years after it happened, in another September. They made me cry.

From person to person, from call to call, in the words people chose to share in their last moments, something seemed to fall away. There were huge fires burning in front of some of them as they made those calls, the rooms they called from swelling with smoke and heat. Some were huddled near the windows, some in the stairwells. Some on the hijacked planes called home from those Airfones that used to be attached to airplane seatbacks and that I remember playing with as a child, pretending to call my dad, or my friend, or my sister. In the face of maybe dying, knowing they might never see the people on the other side of the line on this earth again, there was so often a clarity in the callers' voices, or a peace. They spoke so evenly. They spoke so directly. They spoke so plainly. I see now the thing that struck me most is that they spoke, in the midst of what was happening, so gently. They said, "Hi, baby." They said, "I only have a minute." They calmly explained their circumstance.

Call to call, person to person, voice to voice, they seemed to know at the end what was important. "I love you," they said. "Goodbye," they said. "I hope to be able to see your face again."

I don't remember much from my childhood, but I remember waking from a nap in the dead of winter, snapping awake to find the light of the day had vanished, and that now it was evening. I hadn't meant to fall asleep. I sat up in bed in all my clothes, and I wanted to weep. I can't say why exactly. The house was so quiet. The light outside was the blue of evening, the blue of that movie, *Moonlight*, where the boy stands alone in the dusk, on the abandoned beach, small before the massive sea.

I sat on the edge of my bed, the dark room lit only by the night. The whole upstairs was dark. My parents must have been somewhere, reading quietly or making dinner, but in that moment, staring at the blue window, down into the white yard, filled with snow, I felt alone. I felt the whole world had been emptied, and I'd been left behind.

On that hill in Pennsylvania, in the diminishing light, I felt, again, that emptiness. It was getting late. It made me want to flee that place, to get in my car and drive away, to walk into a crowded bar, to be somewhere surrounded by people. But I was having a hard time leaving. Something was telling me not to rush off. Something in me urged me to try and really see what was around me, or to understand it, somehow, though I'm not exactly sure what I mean. I wanted to be so present in where I was that later in my life, looking back, I wouldn't feel as if I'd simply seen it, but that I'd been there. I guess I felt I was being called to commune, or something, a cosmic beckoning that demanded I wander around this vast cold windblown place, that I remain despite my urge to leave, that I try to think deeply into the past and reckon with what had happened, what role I'd played in what had happened, and what it meant.

If that sounds grand and self-involved, I agree. It makes me think of a story I told Nina once about how, crossing the country on my way to Los Angeles, I'd driven two hours into the desert outside Salt Lake City, set on seeing the Spiral Jetty, a famous land-art installation a friend had told me about.

It had been hot that day, my phone was dying, I'd gotten lost, and when I finally arrived, it wasn't what I had expected: there was a stench from small pools of tar that had seeped up from the pits of the earth, and the jetty was less a spiral and more a curve, like the hook of the handle of an old man's cane. Waterless, with my phone dying, in that heat and emptiness, I walked out along the jetty's path.

Honestly, it was so hot it was hard to breathe. Like, 103 degrees. The air was thick, and despite the demolishing heat, I walked slowly, like a pilgrim in a holy place. I knelt to touch the crust of salt that dusted the ground beneath me. I'd read that in certain years the jetty was unwalkable, entirely submerged in Great Salt Lake's water, but at other times, like the day I found myself there, the heat and relentless beat of the summer sun evaporated the water into the skin of salt I walked on.

As sweat poured off me and my car grew smaller in sight the farther out I walked, as I began to grow dizzy from the sun and blinding heat, the whole time I was saying to myself: *This is what you came for!* Great globs of tar clung to the heels of my sneakers, but still I knelt down to touch the desert floor, thinking smugly of my friends hunched in their air-conditioned living rooms, hypnotized by their sad electronic lives while I was absorbing the silence of God at a Great and Rare Art Installation they'd probably never even see.

The problem was, I wasn't at the Spiral Jetty.

In my revery, I hadn't let myself think too hard about the several cars I'd seen in the hour I was out there drive right past the embankment where I'd turned off. But when I got back to my car, almost shaking now from dehydration, I noticed two or three more vehicles drive right past the embankment. Where could they possibly be going?

In the deepening dusk of the Pennsylvania winter, looking out at the distant lights of the turnpike, I thought of that day in the desert: how I'd gotten back in my car and driven in the direction of the cars that had passed by; how a mile down the road was a paved parking lot packed with vehicles, and a sign welcoming visitors to the Spiral Jetty; how I'd sat there, sick from heat and the mistake I'd made, too fatigued to even leave the car; how I'd driven back to civilization with my tar-crusted sneakers dangling out the open window to keep the car from filling with the smell.

Over the turnpike, the shape of the faraway sun—just a blown-out outline behind the low winter clouds—was sinking. The builders of the memorial had built a long stone walkway that crossed over wetlands and a wide field of wildflowers and ended within viewing distance of the actual crash site, where it was said that the nose of the plane had left a crater thirty feet wide. I followed the walkway, coming closer to where the plane hit, where a boulder that seemed—in the growing darkness—as big as that cube at the center of Mecca had been placed to mark the site of the crash.

It was getting very cold. I imagined Ryan, right then, driving aimlessly through the streets of Columbus, maybe deciding to turn toward home, driving back into the reality of the life that he was living, a life that, in some sense, through our actions in Michigan so many years before, we had played a part in creating.

I was turning over my conversation with Ryan from earlier in the day. I hadn't asked him about Jana. I had intended to. When I woke that morning, I felt I had to at least ask him about her, to mention her name, to give him the space to say something about her, or open up a way for him to do that. In truth, I wanted to discover, too, whether he knew that we'd switched the train schedules that morning in Michigan; if he understood that that was the reason he didn't get home in time to see her audition; if he blamed us.

But I hadn't asked about Jana, and I hadn't had the courage to tell him about our trick. Part of it was cowardice. But part of it, too, was a sense I felt in my heart that it wouldn't do any good. What good could it do for him to know, I asked myself, now that so long had passed?

I was standing in the dusk. The light was vanishing as night fell, so that the great dark boulder in the distance was becoming indistinguishable from the dark wall of woods beyond it. I closed my eyes. I was thinking about a time early in high school, a period of two months, three at the most, that I'd almost forgotten: the warm fall our freshman year, before drinking had made itself an even greater fixture in our lives. If Ben wasn't doing a food drive and David could be pulled away from his mandolin, we'd walk the four blocks east along Fullerton, heading toward the lake, the late-day sun still high and hot. Past Cannon Drive, we'd cross into the shadows and damp of the underpass beneath Lake Shore Drive.

It was wonderful—the sudden coolness of it—the stone walls of the dark tunnel trembling from the river of cars roaring overhead—then the blanket of warmth as we emerged into the heat and the light on the underpass's other side. The lake would be immediately in view, those days so bright the water looked white, shimmering like a plain of salt.

Ryan would never even wait to take his clothes off, would always already be jogging as we left the shadow of the underpass, stripping off his shirt as he picked up speed, leaping, finally, jeans and all, off the stone ledge at the edge of the lake and out into the sparkling blue.

Caesar would follow, then David, Ben, and Neil; and I'd watch them from the rocks—all of them inexplicably tan, their long hair flattened on their foreheads, slapping at one another in the spray—wondering why I didn't have the abandon that they did.

I now can see that even then, I was always worrying about the worst thing that could happen. I had been given this picture book as a kid called *Great Disasters of the World*. It showed images of catastrophes from history: the *Titanic* as it sank; the *Hindenburg* on fire; people leaping from balconies of the MGM Grand in Las Vegas in 1980, trying to escape the blaze. Wherever I was—even there on the rocks as my friends swam in Lake Michigan—I'd look around and think of all the bad things that could happen: a lightning strike; a Jet Ski colliding into one of the guys as they surfaced from a dive; storm waves suddenly rising, piling higher, dragging us out far into the lake.

There in the cold of Pennsylvania, beneath my breath, I counted to ten. I counted from ten down to zero, then from zero back to ten. When I opened my eyes, it was entirely night. My breathing had slowed. I was standing before that long low wall of stone that separated me from the site of the crash, and I reached my hand out to touch it.

Chicago

Not so long after that day, I saw Jana again.

Summer had come; I was visiting Chicago. Sitting at my parents' kitchen table, I saw her name on a brochure from the Art Institute announcing a dance performance that would accompany the opening of a new exhibit. Jana was the choreographer. The photo showed her in a black dress suit and elegant heels, straddling a chair on an otherwise empty stage, the waves of her red hair spilling over her shoulders as she leaned forward toward the camera.

I bought a ticket for the afternoon performance. After it ended, I waited for the crowd to trickle out, then went over to say hello to Jana.

She looked like I remembered: the same spray of freckles around her dark green eyes; the same way, as I'd observed when we were young, she'd tilt her head a little to the side as she listened to someone speak; the same sense that she was truly listening to what you said; the inherent warmth that that communicated. It was the way she was toward everyone.

At a coffee shop on the corner, in the shade of the awning in the hot afternoon, we caught up. She was in Chicago for the summer. She'd been living in Berlin. She was moving in the fall to Vancouver, where she'd gotten a position as an instructor with the Ballet BC.

It was strange to sit with her. Sitting together, listening to her speak, talking with her one-on-one—I realized how seldom we had done that when we were in high school. It was always her with Ryan, or her with the group of us. Back then, I'd preferred it that way. I'd been shy with her. I'd admired her, maybe even desired her. She'd been self-possessed in a way I'd felt I wasn't.

She asked if I remembered putting a colander on my head when we'd been drinking one night in Ryan's kitchen, and wearing it around like a battle helmet.

I laughed and said I didn't remember.

"But it sounds like me," I said.

It made me sad that that was what she remembered of me. I'd spent so much time observing her and Ryan. Back then, when we were in high school, I'd always hoped she saw my quiet not as emptiness, but as a sign of a rich inner life, that I was someone worth being interested in.

She asked me about Caesar, about David and Neil, about Ben and Ricky. I asked her about Ryan. She shrugged.

"He wrote me a letter once," Jana said. "Five, six years ago maybe."

What had it said?

"He said hello. He said he thinks of me."

Then she laughed.

"He said he looks for me in airports, actually."

"What do you mean?"

"Every time he flies," she said. "Every time he arrives in a new airport; he said he can't help it. He said he finds himself thinking he might see me there."

I pictured Ryan stepping off a plane, the hope entering his mind that he might unexpectedly run into Jana; buying a coffee or reading a magazine, waiting for his connecting flight, searching for her face in the crowd of passing people. It made my heart ache for him.

"Did you write him back?" I asked.

She shook her head.

"No," she said. "I kept sitting down to, but I didn't know what I would say."

I swirled the silt of ice and coffee around the bottom of my cup. I was thinking about Ryan, of Ryan arriving in Charlotte, or Fresno, or Reno, or Anchorage, the lonely cities his job as a marine recruiter took him to, his hope of seeing her. He'd been on the road, before he had his daughter, for thirty weeks a year. I thought of the miles and miles of identical gray concourse carpet, Ryan always absently on the lookout for Jana, for a flash of her hair, her expression impassive among the passing strangers, that blaze of genuine earnestness that would color her face when she looked up and recognized him, so different than he'd been those last times she saw him, now in his crisp blue uniform, his shoulders wide and firm beneath his jacket.

I saw a movie once where this high-profile investment banker gets a glimpse of his life as it might have been. In the life he didn't take, he works in a tire shop; he marries his high school sweetheart, the prettiest girl in the county; they share a beer on the couch, then make love right there on the living room floor; he bowls on Sundays with his friends. When he's returned by an angel to the life he lives, he longs for the life in the glimpse he's been given. He drives to the airport. He stops the woman he loves at the gate, before she boards. He tries to explain. He tells her about their daughters, the Italian place he always takes her for dinner on her birthday, the way that they spend Christmas, the life they might have shared together. She looks at him in disbelief. He convinces her to have a cup of coffee with him, just one, to hear him out. She shrugs. She does. She lets her flight depart without her. That's where the movie leaves them.

"Graham," Jana said.

I looked up at her. It startled me to hear her speak my name.

"How are you?" she asked.

The question froze me. I hadn't been expecting it, or, I hadn't thought of how I was. To tell the truth of that, to determine it, seemed so complex, even to myself.

I was still living in Philadelphia; I was living alone, though not without happiness, or at least without some meaning. I volunteered. I still didn't sleep well. I went to see my godson every six weeks, in New Haven or Long Island. He loved trucks, any kind at all, and I brought him one each time. I'd returned to the writing in the journals that I'd kept. What had begun as little sketches, descriptions, images, and memories, I had started expanding into fuller stories. In writing them I'd discovered something that I love: examining the past, going back inside of time and trying to better understand. It may be true that in revisiting the past I feel I understand more, but it is equally true that the more of the past that I examine, the more there seems to yet be understood.

"I'm good," I said.

Hearing myself speak those words, the emptiness of that answer, I remembered that day on Long Island, playing beer pong with Caesar, answering that same question the exact same way.

"I'm fine," I added. I told her I was writing.

"What are you writing?" she asked.

I told her I was writing this.

"What is it about?" she asked.

When I explained, she was perplexed. She was surprised to find herself and Ryan so closely at its center.

"Why would you tell that story?" she asked me. The sun was sinking. Jana brushed the crumbs from the table, then scooted her chair back a bit. I sensed she was ready to leave. "I haven't thought about what happened in high school for a very long time," she continued. "I'm happy," she told me. She told me she imagined Ryan was happy too. When she thought about what happened between them, she didn't see it as a tragedy. "It's just what happened," she said. "It's just something that happened."

I've thought about that conversation ever since. Sometimes I think their story was a tragedy—that it is—our actions preventing a life between Ryan and Jana, a life that might have been.

But at other times I think of Sam. I think, on those days, how if Ryan had never lost Jana, perhaps he never would have enlisted in the marines. Had he not enlisted, had he not gone off to war, it's possible that he never would have gotten sober. Had he not gotten sober, who would've been there that day that Sam left the hospital? Who would have helped her? What would have happened—as she sat there in an empty bar on that cold afternoon and sent that message asking for help—if Ryan hadn't been there to answer? Perhaps, because of the strange chain of events we set in motion that day we switched the timetables, it saved her life.

I think of David and Sofia asking me to be the godfather to their son. I think of Nina, though it's been years since we've spoken, alive in Los Angeles, making her paintings, walking along Pacific Avenue at dusk, turning toward the ocean.

I think of Sam, working in New Jersey as a nurse, sober now for almost thirteen years. On good days, when I think of them, it makes me believe in something invisible that has been there all along, running like a river through our lives—calm, steady, benevolent, so familiar as to be almost imperceptible. It's a thought that comforts me.

Jana got up to leave. I stood up as she did and reached out my hand to pass her her purse, but she wasn't looking, so I continued to hold it, the black strap warm from the sun, and I let it hang from my hand as I walked her to the train.

"Well," she said, when we got there.

"Well," I said, turning to face her, thinking she was going to say something.

But she just gave a little nod toward my hand.

"Oh, right," I said. The purse.

A tiny green leaf had landed on it as we'd sat at the table, or as we'd walked, and I picked it from a crease in the black leather, then handed her the bag.

"Thanks," she said.

And then she stepped forward and hugged me, and held me for a beat, and let me go. And then she said goodbye.

After Jana left, I stood on the street corner for a little while. Traffic passed back and forth. Music played from the open windows of passing cars. It was July. In the park across the street, children ran across the paths, calling out to one another through the dusk.

I saw, down the street, the lights of a movie theater's glowing marquee, and went in to see a film whose ending continues to haunt me. It follows the protagonist from his boyhood in Florida to his adulthood in Georgia. Like me, he was meek. Like me, he did not act on life, but let life act on him, like a boulder on the face of a high mountain, its shape warped by continuous wind. By the film's end the boy has grown into a man, but the last shot is of his face as the unformed boy he's always been, standing on a bare beach in the evening on the shore, looking out into the dark.

A Note on Historical Accuracy

This novel references a number of historical events, texts, and places. In depicting them in the novel, I have departed from a strictly factual account in order to best fit this story, its characters, and its fictional timeline.

If you're interested in nonfiction accounts of some of the events described in *Great Disasters*, I encourage you to seek out the following books:

A Stranger in Your Own City: Travels in the Middle East's Long War, by Ghaith Abdul-Ahad

The Forever War, by Dexter Filkins

The Sixties: Years of Hope, Days of Rage, by Todd Gitlin

All the Devils Are Here: The Hidden History of the Financial Crisis, by Bethany McLean and Joe Nocera

The Unwinding: An Inner History of the New America, by George Packer

Daring to Struggle, Daring to Win, by Helen Shiller

The Afghanistan Papers: A Secret History of the War, by Craig Whitlock

Bush at War; *Plan of Attack: The Definitive Account of the Decision to Invade Iraq*; *State of Denial: Bush at War, Part III*; and *The War Within: A Secret White House History 2006–2008*, all by Bob Woodward

Films Referenced

The films referenced in this book are as follows, with the caveat that the narrator's descriptions of them are more impressionistic than literal, and are not always entirely accurate to certain scenes within them. In some cases, the narrator makes reference to films that are either wholly invented or are a compilation of memories of different films. I hope you'll forgive the liberties I've taken and that you'll see the films themselves, each of which has stayed with me and informed the world of this story. I am grateful for and indebted to all those who played a part in their creation.

p. 3: The movie loosely referenced here is *Little Women* (1994), directed by Gillian Armstrong. The screenplay is by Robin Swicord and is based on the 1868 semi-autobiographical novel by Louisa May Alcott.

pp. 6–7: *Graduate First* (*Passe ton bac d'abord* in the French, 1978), written and directed by Maurice Pialat.

p. 13: *Summertime* (1955), directed by David Lean, screenplay by David Lean, H. E. Bates, and Donald Ogden Stewart.

pp. 16-7: *Breakfast at Tiffany's* (1961), directed by Blake Edwards. The screenplay is by George Axelrod and is based on the 1958 novella of the same name by Truman Capote.

p. 19: *The 400 Blows* (*Les quatre cents coups* in the French, 1959), directed by François Truffaut, screenplay by François Truffaut and Marcel Moussy.

p. 31: *The Visitor* (2007), written and directed by Tom McCarthy.

p. 31: *Paranoid Park* (2007), written and directed by Gus Van Sant, based on the novel of the same name by Blake Nelson.

p. 31: *The Other Boleyn Girl* (2008), directed by Justin Chadwick. The screenplay is by Peter Morgan and is based off Philippa Gregory's 2001 novel of the same name.

p. 31: *My Blueberry Nights* (2007), directed by Wong Kar-wai, story by Wong Kar-wai, screenplay by Wong Kar-wai and Lawrence Block.

pp. 62–3: *Cruel Intentions* (1999), directed by Roger Kumble, screenplay by Roger Kumble.

p. 64: *The Fog of War: Eleven Lessons from the Life of Robert S. McNamara* (2003), directed by Errol Morris.

p. 85: *Fanny and Alexander* (*Fanny och Alexander* in the Swedish, 1982), directed by Ingmar Bergman, screenplay by Ingmar Bergman.

p. 87: *It Happened One Night* (1934), directed by Frank Capra in collaboration with Harry Cohn, screenplay by Robert Riskin.

p. 94: *Save the Last Dance* (2001), directed by Thomas Carter, screenplay by Duane Adler and Cheryl Edwards.

p. 94: *Amadeus* (1984), directed by Miloš Forman. The screenplay is by Peter Shaffer and is adapted from his 1979 stage play of the same name, in turn inspired by the 1830 play *Mozart and Salieri* by Alexander Pushkin.

p. 119: *Wonder Boys* (2000), directed by Curtis Hanson. The screenplay is by Steve Kloves and is based on the 1995 novel of the same name by Michael Chabon.

p. 119: *Almost Famous* (2000), directed by Cameron Crowe, screenplay by Cameron Crowe.

pp. 119–20: *My Life as a Dog* (*Mitt liv som hund* in the Swedish, 1985), directed by Lasse Hallström. The screenplay is by Lasse Hallström, Reidar Jönsson, Brasse Brännström, and Per Berglund and is based on the 1983 semi-autobiographical novel of the same name by Reidar Jönsson.

p. 147: *Call Me by Your Name* (2017), directed by Luca Guadagnino. The screenplay is by James Ivory and is based on the 2007 novel of the same name by André Aciman.

p. 182: *The Purge: Election Year* (2016), directed by James DeMonaco, screenplay by James DeMonaco.

pp. 185 and 198: *Moonlight* (2016), directed by Barry Jenkins. The screenplay is by Barry Jenkins and is based on Tarell Alvin McCraney's unpublished semi-autobiographical play, *In Moonlight Black Boys Look Blue*.

pp. 195–6: *The Family Man* (2000), directed by Brett Ratner, screenplay by David Diamond and David Weissman.

Additional Works Referenced

p. 30: Hersh, Seymour M. "The Iran Plans." *The New Yorker*, April 9, 2006. https://www.newyorker.com/magazine/2006/04/17/the-iran-plans.

p. 43: The Holy Bible: King James Version, Matthew 5:5. The quote referenced is "Blessed are the meek: for they shall inherit the earth."

pp. 59–60: Fukuyama, Francis. "The End of History?" *The National Interest*, no. 16 (Summer 1989): 3-18.

p. 70: The dance move referenced here is called a "prisiadka," defined by *Merriam-Webster* as, "a Slavic male dance step executed by extending the legs alternately forward from a squatting position."

p. 123: The song referenced is "Wish You Were Here," by Pink Floyd, from their 1975 album of the same name.

p. 128: Cave, Damien. "In Florida, Despair and Foreclosures." *The New York Times*, February 7, 2009. https://www.nytimes.com/2009/02/08/us/08lehigh.html.

pp. 154–5: Joyce, James. *Ulysses*, 1st ed. Vintage International, 1990. The passage about Rudy appears on p. 285 of this edition; the passage about the two hats on p. 88.

pp. 184–5: Hurley, Bevan. "'I'm so thankful for that message': The Final Phone Calls from the Twin Towers." *The Independent*, September 9, 2022. https://www.independent.co.uk/news/world/americas/9-11final-calls-twin-towers-b2163982.html.

National Park Service. "Phone Calls from Flight 93." Last updated June 24, 2023. https://www.nps.gov/flni/learn/historyculture/phone-calls-from-flight-93.htm

National Commission on Terrorist Attacks Upon the United States. *The 9/11 Commission Report: Final Report of the National Commission on Terrorist Attacks Upon the United States*. Washington, D.C.: U.S. Government Printing Office, 2004.

p. 189: Frank, Beryl. *Great Disasters of the World*. Galahad Books, 1981.

Acknowledgments

For their conversation, encouragement, and support in the work of this book: Halley Chambers, Scott Chambers, Eric Lach, Emily Marie Reynolds, Jessica Scicchitano, Steve Koteff, and Annie Liontas.

My deepest appreciation and gratitude to Elizabeth DeMeo for believing in this book, and for her editorial insight and wisdom, which did so much to help it become.

To the Tin House team of Masie Cochran, Beth Steidle, Becky Kraemer, Nanci McCloskey, Jacqui Reiko Teruya, Isabel Lemus Kristensen, Justine Payton, and to out-of-house copyeditor Meg Storey and proofreader Lisa Dusenbery: thank you, thank you.

For the inspiration and example of their writing, and for their support of this book: Dana Spiotta, Christine Schutt, Chris Beha, Jim Shepard, and Amber Caron.

Tim Craven and Adam Bright, for their steadfast friendship and conversations around writing, and Joey McGarvey, for wise counsel.

To my oldest friends, for who (whom!) something of the world and spirit of this book will feel familiar—my love and gratitude.

And for my mom, Marilyn Katz, in love and memory.

EMILY MARIE REYNOLDS

Grady Chambers is the author of the poetry collection *North American Stadiums* (Milkweed Editions, 2018), winner of the Max Ritvo Poetry Prize. Grady was born and raised on the north side of Chicago, and lives in Philadelphia. His writing can be found in *The Atlantic*, *The Paris Review*, *American Poetry Review*, *The Sun*, and many other publications. Grady is a former Wallace Stegner Fellow, and received his MFA in Creative Writing from Syracuse University. More info at gradychambers.com.